HARTSVILLE'S SEAL HEROES

The SEAL's Convenient Wife

The SEAL's Surprise Baby

The SEAL's Instant Family

The SEAL's Pregnant Roommate

The SEAL's Treatment

The SEAL's Hookup

RELAY
PUBLISHING

The SEAL'S Pregnant Roommate

HARTSVILLE'S SEAL HEROES BOOK FOUR

USA TODAY BESTSELLING AUTHOR

LESLIE NORTH

BLURB

Can these two lonely souls catch a lucky break in love?

Harley Von's never been lucky in life, let alone in love. And her streak of ill fortune continues when her long-lost brother passes away just as they were on the verge of reconnecting. On the run from a bad relationship, she's less than delighted to find herself sharing Sebastian's fixer-upper with his gruff but gorgeous friend, Garrett. With her ex breathing down her neck and a baby on the way, Harley's got plenty to deal with. Falling for a sexy SEAL isn't part of her plan.

Navy SEAL Garrett Moore isn't looking for romance. His life is the SEALs, end of discussion. Still, grieving and guilt-ridden over his teammate's death, he's determined to do what he can to help Sebastian's sister. And Harley's combination of vulnerability and determination is captivating. She's like a skittish fawn refusing to back down from a mountain lion.

He can't help feeling protective of her, especially when the ex shows up and gets physical. But Garrett's only in town for as long as it takes to repair the old house.

Love has a funny way of changing things, though

MAILING LIST

Thank you for reading "The SEAL's Pregnant Roommate"
(Hartsville's SEAL Heroes Book Four)

Read FIVE full-length romances by USA Today best-selling author Leslie North for FREE! Over 600+ pages of best-selling romance with hundreds of FIVE STAR REVIEWS!

Sign-up to her mailing list and get your FREE books:
www.leslienorthbooks.com/sign-up-for-free-books

CONTENTS

PROLOGUE

Garrett raised his glass. "To Sebastian," he said before downing the shot of whiskey. He knew he should say more to honor his best friend, but after giving the eulogy at that morning's funeral, in a quiet cemetery in Sebastian's hometown, he felt drained of words.

Their jobs were risky. As SEALs, he, Sebastian, and the other five men gathered in the back room of the Main Street Tavern accepted that they could be killed or injured in the line of duty. His gaze fell on his buddy Matthew's hand, still in bandages as the burns and broken bones from the same mission that took Sebastian's life continued to heal. Paying the ultimate price was always a possibility, but that didn't stop it from hurting the ones who were left behind. Particularly the one who felt—painfully, down deep—that he should have prevented it, should have found a way to save his closest friend.

"I want to thank you all for sticking around to toast Sebastian." Now that the funeral and the formalities were over, it was time for the SEAL tradition of gathering around to commemorate the fallen and share stories of the deceased.

"Got a memory to share?" Patrick asked. He was one of three SEALs who also called Hartsville, South Carolina, home. Patrick, Anderson, and Kenton were a few years older than Garrett and served on a different team than Garrett, Matthew, Jonathan, and Sebastian, but brothers in arms shared a common bond.

"Yeah. Hard to pick which one, to be honest." Garrett twirled the empty shot glass between his fingers. "Sebastian and I go back almost ten years. Teammates, friends. You know the drill. But I saw another side of him when we were working on his house on Lake Hart. There's something about taking a crowbar to old plaster walls at three in the morning that brings out a person's true nature. Sebastian could be a dreamer, with all these pie-in-the-sky ideas for what he could do with that broken-down old wreck. I laughed at him when he first showed it to me, telling him he'd been hosed if he'd paid more than five bucks for the place, but he just shook his head and told me that he saw what it could become. Sebastian always knew how to see the potential in things, how to bring out the best—in everything and everyone."

Because he'd do anything for his best friend, Garrett had signed on to help bring those dreams to life. As a teen, Garrett had spent his summers working for his dad, who was a contractor, so he'd volunteered to help out in exchange for a place to live between missions. He'd always have good memories of working with Sebastian on it. It put another little crack in his heart that Sebastian would never see the home complete, fully restored.

Garrett chuckled over something that happened the week before they'd left for the mission. "I kept thumping my head on the floor joists down in the basement, so Sebastian painted them fluorescent orange. Can't miss 'em now."

"Wouldn't have needed to do that if you weren't so damn tall," Matthew teased, and the others laughed. At three inches over six feet,

Garrett was on the tall side for a SEAL, which made his job a challenge at times in tight quarters. "But yeah, doesn't surprise me that Sebastian found a way to fix it for you. He was always doing that—for all of us. He saved my ass plenty of times, and not just in the field. Years back, I bought a used Harley from a guy who was getting out of the service. I drove it around base for a few days and it seemed to run fine, so I figured it was good to go. I hopped on and headed north across the Chesapeake Bay Bridge. It was getting late, and I should have turned back, but I was enjoying the ride… right up until the bike died on a country road in the middle of nowhere, Virginia, after eleven at night. So I called Sebastian. He brought me enough gas to get back to base and followed behind me all the way to make sure I did. Turned out the gas gauge didn't work."

"Bet he helped you fix the bike, too," Jonathan said.

"Yeah, the next day. You're up next." Matthew reached for the bottle of whiskey with his good hand and poured everyone another shot.

"Sebastian saved my bacon plenty over the years, but my best memory of him was right here on Lake Hart. We were on leave after a mission in Afghanistan. It had been a rough one." Jonathan paused, seeming to gather himself.

Garrett remembered that mission. What they saw go down at an elementary school still haunted him. He'd gone home to Idaho for two weeks to see his family and hug his nieces and nephews. As their team leader, Jonathan surely felt the losses of those they couldn't save even more than Garrett did.

"Anyway," Jonathan continued. "Sebastian dragged me home with him. We hung out on his boat, drank beer, pretended to fish, and just talked. It helped." He smiled. "We did manage to catch a few trout, and they were damn tasty when we fried them up. Shit, I'm going to miss him. To Sebastian." This time, Jonathan raised his glass in a toast.

"I wish we all could have known him as well as you guys did," Anderson said. "My first memory of him was seeing him working at a little local barbecue stand in the summer. Sebastian was skinny and gangly, but not half bad with a football." He gestured between himself, Patrick, and Kenton. "We were all in high school at the time, but we could see he was talented."

"That's right," Kenton said. "I saw him play at the Naval Academy. He was damn good."

"You got that right, and good-hearted, too," Patrick added. "Did you know he helped build the new playground behind the elementary school?" Garrett remembered that Patrick's wife was a teacher there. "Pretty unusual to have four Navy SEALs working on a community project, especially in a town this size."

"I always told Sebastian there must be something special in the water around here," Garrett said. "That's a lot of SEALs to come out of one small town."

"We grow 'em tough around here." Patrick grinned and flexed his arms, making them all laugh.

"That must be true," Garrett agreed.

"So… for those of us who weren't there, what the hell happened?" Kenton asked after the laughter died down. The question didn't surprise Garrett. It wasn't an easy subject, but Sebastian's other friends deserved to have the details—and they had the security clearance to get the full story. He glanced at Matthew and Jonathan. They were all struggling with the aftermath of the flawed mission in different ways.

"It was a shitshow," Matthew said. "You tell it, Garrett."

Garrett didn't want to, but he would, to save his teammates from having to recount the details. "We were tasked with taking down the leader of a drug cartel in Colombia. We'd been gathering intel for over a month, and we'd narrowed the window to take the guy out and confiscate the drugs. We settled on a day for the raid—but the day after the decision was made, and two days before it was scheduled to actually happen, Sebastian and I were on recon, and we realized that the guy was getting ready to rabbit. He knew we were on to him. He'd been tipped off. I don't know by who."

"I made the decision to move the raid up." Jonathan took over the story. "His connections were too good. He'd have been in the wind."

The other SEALs all nodded. It wasn't unusual to adjust time frames based on new intel, but it was always a risk, since so much depended on careful planning.

"Sebastian and I had spent the night doing recon, so we'd been up for over twenty-four hours, but I didn't like the thought of the team going in without me. I made the decision to go on the raid, and Sebastian went with me." Garrett thought about those moments. They'd both known they should catch some shut-eye, but Garrett had insisted on being included.

If you're going, I'm going, bro. I've got your back. Sebastian's words would stick with him forever. Garrett could have made a different choice. If he had, his friend would still be alive. But that wasn't how it played out.

"I needed every man," Jonathan said. "Every man I could trust, that is." There were still unanswered questions about who tipped off the cartel. Garrett agreed with Jonathan's conclusion that it had to be someone on their SEAL team. Whoever it was, they had blood on their hands and one hell of a lot to answer for.

"The raid was a shitshow from the start." Garrett picked back up the narrative. "The compound was full of people, mostly civilians who were forced to live and work there, processing the drugs. They panicked as soon as they saw us. It was total chaos." He looked to Matthew, who gave him a nod before speaking.

"I was checking for mines and other explosives as the rest of the team worked to secure the site. I found a bomb that I knew I wouldn't be able to defuse before it detonated. We had to move, and fast, but people were running everywhere, trying to get away from us, not listening to our warnings that they needed to get out of the building." Matthew ducked his head and fiddled with the bandage on his hand. He hadn't run. He'd stayed working on the bomb until the last second, resulting in injuries that might cost him his career. An explosions expert needed his hands in flawless working order—and that might not be achievable. No one was sure if he would be fit for active duty again.

"We'd evacuated our team and as many civilians as we could… but then Sebastian went back in," Garrett said, wanting to get the worst of it over. "He thought he might be able to get through to those last civilians before the bomb detonated. He didn't make it out in time."

There was nothing Garrett could do now to change the outcome, but that didn't mean he wouldn't carry the burden the rest of his life.

"That sucks, man," Patrick said with a glance at his own teammates. "Is there anything we can do to help? Does he have any living family? I didn't see any at the funeral."

"I understand that Sebastian had recently reconnected with his sister," Kenton said. "What's the deal there?"

Garrett knew that all he had to do was ask, and the five men with him would do whatever they could for Sebastian's sister. He just wasn't sure what she needed, since he hadn't met her yet. "I don't know much. Her name's Harley Von. Their mom died when they were little, and she and Sebastian were placed in foster care."

"They got separated?" Patrick asked.

"Different dads, different last names, so any plans for keeping them together fell through the cracks. Sebastian was always looking for her, though—hired a PI and everything once he was able to get the records unsealed. About two months ago, he found her in Florida. They communicated via email and chatted on Zoom once, while we were on the mission." Sebastian had been so excited about locating his only sibling. He'd talked nonstop about getting to see her once they got back to the States. "He told me that he'd changed his will to make her his beneficiary. I don't know what all that entails, but he wanted to do what he could for her. He had the impression that she was in a bad relationship, but he didn't share the details with me. Sebastian's lawyer told me that she's coming in a few days for the reading of the will. I guess she wasn't able to make it for the funeral."

"Tough break," Anderson commented. "Find your brother and lose him that fast. If she needs anything, you let us know."

"I will." Though he planned on doing as much as he could himself. It was the least he could do for Sebastian. Garrett would stick around long enough to make sure that Harley was set, and then he'd head on out of Hartsville. He liked the place, but it was a family town, and he'd never been interested in finding the right woman and settling down. He had to respect the guys like Patrick, Kenton, and Anderson, who somehow balanced their careers as SEALs with having wives and kids, but that kind of life wasn't for him. The way he saw it, he was married to the Navy.

"I'd better head back," Jonathan said, standing. "I've got more questions to face." The brass were demanding answers about everything that had gone wrong on the mission, which probably explained why he'd drunk only one shot in Sebastian's memory.

"Yeah." Matthew got to his feet as well. "And I want to see what the docs say about this." He held up his hand. "Take care, Garrett. Keep us posted on how things go."

"Will do." Garrett walked the rest of the men out and watched them leave after shaking hands and giving hugs all around. He'd see his teammates back on base soon enough, but until then… that was going to be the tough part. He'd be living in Sebastian's house, continuing the work they'd planned together, but his buddy was never going to walk through the door. Somehow, Garrett was going to have to come to terms with that. And with the fact that it was his fault.

1

"Hello, I'm Harley Von." A woman's voice, soft and uncertain, reached Garrett through the open door as he waited in Sebastian's lawyer's office. "I'm here to see Mr. Burke for a will reading."

Garrett sat up a little straighter. So here was the mysterious Harley, just a few feet away and heading toward him. Damn, he wished he weren't meeting Sebastian's sister under these circumstances. Why the hell couldn't Sebastian have lived to welcome her to his home? The fact that he'd never get to reconnect with Harley made his death an even bigger tragedy.

"Yes, hello. He had to step out to take an urgent call, but you can wait in his office," the receptionist said. "He'll be right in. The other party involved is already inside. Can I get you coffee or tea?"

"No, thank you. I'm fine. Through here?" Why did her voice sound so timid? Was she naturally soft-spoken… or had Sebastian been right to think that she was in a bad relationship?

"That's right, honey. Just take a seat."

Garrett stood and turned toward the door, not sure what to expect. Would Harley look like Sebastian? He steeled himself to find out.

Damn, she did. Dark hair, tanned skin, full lips, and wide brown eyes that met his for a second before turning downward. It was long enough for him to recognize those eyes. They were just like Sebastian's—same size, shape, color. But they lacked the warmth and friendship Sebastian's had always held. In their place was a wariness bordering on fear.

Harley was above average height for a woman, but slim, almost too thin. He studied her face. She'd carefully applied makeup, but it looked like she had a bruise near her left eye. His concerns about that relationship ratcheted up.

"Ms. Von," he said. "I'm Garrett Moore. I served with your brother and considered him my closest friend." He held out his hand, and she shook it so quickly that he barely felt the press of her fingers before they were withdrawn. "Maybe you should sit?" He didn't want to order her to, but he feared that if she didn't, she'd either run or faint.

"Thank you. And please, call me Harley." She took the chair next to his, discreetly scooting it a little farther away, and quickly crossed her legs. Long legs that her black skirt showed plenty of. He yanked his eyes away, reminding himself that this wasn't the time or place and definitely not the person he should be noticing in that way. Focusing on her face, he watched as she nervously tucked her long hair behind her ear and then pulled it forward again. Was she trying to conceal the bruise?

"I'm so sorry about your brother," Garrett said.

She gave him a brief glance. "I'm sorry for you, too, if you were his friend. I wish I could have made it to his funeral. I… I wanted to."

"His SEAL team was here. And others who knew him. Do you want to hear about it?" he asked. He didn't want to relive the funeral, but she deserved to hear the details, if she wanted them.

"Please."

He talked for a few minutes about Matthew and Jonathan, the 21-gun salute, and the playing of Taps, making sure to emphasize how respected and loved Sebastian had been. When the lawyer still failed to return, he kept going and told her about Patrick and his wife Imogen, Anderson and Violet, and Kenton and Mia. If Harley was going to stay in Hartsville, she'd want friends, and his fellow SEALS and their wives were a good place to start. He knew they'd be more than happy to step up and help her feel at home.

"Thank you for being there," she said when he was done, and he fought to hide a flinch. She shouldn't thank him. If she knew what had happened, the responsibility he bore for her brother's death, she might curse him. He doubted that, though, since she seemed sweet. He wanted to say the right thing to her, but he didn't know what that was. Before he figured out how to reply, the lawyer entered the room.

"Sorry about that," the man said before stepping over to Harley. "Anthony Burke, attorney at law. You must be Ms. Von?" When she nodded, he reached out to shake her hand. Garrett felt the tiniest bit better when she didn't hold on to the lawyer's hand for any longer than she'd held his. "I'm very sorry for your loss. Thank you for coming all this way for the will reading. I don't want to drag this out. Dealing with the death of any family member is difficult, but it's even harder when it's so unexpected. Shall we get started?"

"That would be appreciated," Garrett answered for himself and Harley, who only gave a nod.

Burke sat behind his desk and opened a folder. He pulled several papers from it and spread them out. "The terms of Sebastian Valenti's will are pretty straightforward. All SEALs are required to have an updated will on file at the base, but your brother took the additional step of having a signed original here in Hartsville as well."

Garrett cast a glance at Harley. She looked even more fragile than earlier.

"Would you like me to do the official reading or cut through the legal language to provide an overview?" Burke asked.

"Just give me the synopsis, please," she said.

"In short, Sebastian left everything to you, with Garrett Moore as the executor." Burke turned his attention to one page in particular, which appeared to list the assets. "By everything, I mean his home on the lake here in Hartsville—including the boat docked there—his car, the funds in his bank accounts, and his investments. He specifically named an investment that he'd made in a friend's start-up company with the note that he hoped you would continue to support the business."

"Oh," she breathed.

"Here are copies of the most recent bank and investment account statements." He handed over a sheaf of papers.

"I hadn't expected…" She bit her lower lip as she trailed off.

"Your brother was a man who managed his income well." Burke's tone was gentle. "You'll also receive his life insurance and the death benefits from the Navy. All of that is in order." He caught Garrett's eye and nodded to an open box on the edge of his desk. "Mr. Moore, if you'd like to…"

Garrett had placed the box there when he'd first entered the office, so he wasn't surprised at Burke's request. He took the box, knowing that what was in it would be difficult for Harley to see.

"Harley. The Navy gives a flag to the next of kin during a military funeral. I accepted it on your behalf. It's in here along with Sebastian's service medals and official portrait. If you'd rather not look at them now—"

"No, I'd like to," she said, drawing herself up. She still didn't make eye contact with him, but she was staring at the box as if it were the most valuable thing in the world. "I only ever saw him on that one Zoom—I mean, since we were kids—and I can't remember what he looked like clearly. I was only six when we were separated."

Garrett pulled out the portrait taken two years earlier and handed it to her. She studied it carefully for several seconds, running her fingers over the glass. Garrett had many more photographs of Sebastian on his phone. He'd show those to her and tell her stories about her brother before he returned to base, so she could get a better sense of Sebastian. She deserved that.

"There's a note for you as well. It came in an email to me. Would you like me to read it?" the lawyer asked. When she nodded, Burke started with the date: just two weeks before Sebastian's death. He would have already been in Colombia, prepping for the mission.

"'If you're reading this, it means I'm gone. I'm so sorry, Sis. I'd hoped that we'd have more time, that we'd be able to really get to know each other, but it looks like it wasn't meant to be. I want you to know how much it means to me that I finally found you. Please know that I love you, and I've kept you in my heart.'"

Burke paused when Harley let out a soft sob, but she waved for him to continue. Garrett wanted to take her hand and give her what comfort he could, but she didn't look as if she'd welcome being touched.

"'I know that I'm not leaving you alone, since my best friend, Garrett, should be sitting by your side. If you need anything, ask him. I mean that. There's no one in the world I trust more. I hope you have a happy life, Harley. I'm sorry I won't be there to share it. All my love, Sebastian.'"

Garrett felt his friend's words deep in his soul. Sebastian had trusted him, but Garrett had failed him in the end. He hadn't forced Sebastian to join him on that raid, but when he'd volunteered for it, he had known that Sebastian would, as well. They'd always done everything together. If one of them went, the other did, too.

Except now. Garrett was alone, but he could honor Sebastian's memory by helping his sister. He'd do what he could for her.

"Is there anything else?" she asked, seeming anxious to leave the office.

"Just a small delay for you to be aware of. The will has to go through probate, but due to the rotation of the court, we just missed the visit from the circuit court judge. He comes back around to our courthouse in four weeks. I hope that won't be too much of a problem. Garrett has access to the house, as well as the boat and car. You can take immediate possession of those, though you won't be able to sell anything until the estate is settled. The only issue is with the financial accounts. I'm afraid you won't be able to get into those until the judge returns."

"That's fine, as long as I have a place to live for now." She stood. "Thank you both." With that, she took the packet of papers and the box and headed for the door.

Garrett caught up with her on the street as she was getting into an older Buick sedan. "Harley. Wait a minute." She gave him a nervous look as he approached. "You don't know where the house is. I assume you want to go there."

"I do. Isn't the address in the papers?" She was still clutching them.

"Probably, but the roads out by the lake can be confusing if you're not familiar with the town. Why don't you follow me?"

She didn't answer right away as she glanced down the street. Hartsville had an old-fashioned downtown with brick-fronted buildings that housed small businesses. Did she like what she saw here? He did, even if it wasn't home to him. He hoped it would be to her. Being in Hartsville might give her the fresh start he had a feeling she needed.

"Sebastian trusted you. I guess I can, too," she said after a minute, but she didn't sound convinced of it.

Out here in the daylight, it was easier to see past her makeup job to the full, nasty extent of the bruise. It looked to be the kind that happens when someone's fist connects with a face. It was on the tip of his tongue to ask about it, but he didn't know her well enough yet. Despite that, every protective nerve in his body fired at rapid speed. He'd help anyone in trouble, but there was something more about Harley herself that drew Garrett in. He told himself that it was just because she was Sebastian's sister… but deep down, he wondered if it was something more.

2

———

Harley followed Garrett's truck, aware of her trembling hands. Hearing Sebastian's will and the note from him had been almost too much for her, and she'd struggled to keep from breaking down. The lawyer and Garrett had been kind, but she desperately wanted to be alone. She might… might feel safe then.

Garrett turned down a driveway lined with pine trees and came to a stop in front of a home. As she stepped out of her car, she had to admit that the property her brother left her wasn't quite what she expected. The house had good bones and clearly had the potential to be a showpiece, but it was very obviously under renovation. A dumpster sat next to the house, and she could see a carpentry station near it.

She tried to ignore all that and focus on the structure. It had to be at least a hundred years old, based on the wraparound porch and steeply peaked roof. Long, narrow windows and a double door graced the front entry. Oh, yes, it could be lovely. And it was hers. That was going to take some time to sink in.

She stepped to the side, where she could see into the backyard and to the lake beyond. Lake Hart, if she remembered correctly from when she looked up the town. And there was a boat—the lawyer had mentioned that. Not that she had any idea how to drive one, but she saw it bobbing at the end of the dock. There was even a little structure, a sort of summerhouse, built where the dock connected to the land.

This could be peaceful. And safe, she thought. A safe place for her to be while she filed for divorce from Thomas and waited for that process to play out. She rubbed a finger near her left eye where one of the bruises from the final time he'd beaten her remained. She had other marks on her upper arms and thighs, but those were covered by her clothing.

Thank goodness he hadn't kicked her in the stomach this time. He enjoyed doing that: knocking her to the floor and pummeling her with his feet. She'd been lucky—his phone had rung, distracting him. He'd taken the call, instantly turning on the facade of the charming man she thought she'd fallen in love with. That man was a far cry from the monster she'd lived with in recent months.

Never again, she told herself. Never again would anyone do that to her. She'd soon be free of Thomas. Free to live here and raise her child where no one could harm either of them.

"Pop your trunk, and I'll get your luggage."

She spun around to face Garrett. Why had he gotten out of his truck? She had the house key. She had no need of his help, and she didn't want him around. He was large, tall, and intimidating. She swallowed hard. He was handsome, too, in a rugged way, with his white-blond hair and green eyes. But she wasn't drawn in by that. Good looks didn't mean he had a good character. Thomas had taught her that lesson. Painfully.

"No need," she said. "Thanks for your help, but I can handle it from here."

He hesitated. "I guess it wasn't clear at the lawyer's office. I've been living in the house while doing renovation work on it. That was my deal with Sebastian—labor in exchange for free rent. And I've continued with the work since… since I returned from the mission."

"The one he died on?" No one had given her any details of Sebastian's death except to say it happened somewhere in South America.

"That's right."

"So you were there?"

He dipped his chin. She could ask for more information. But did she want to know? Maybe. Someday. She had other things to deal with first, like getting this man to understand that she preferred to be alone. "I would like to know more about… all that, but not today. I just want to get settled."

"Look." He lifted his hands, and she instinctively took a step back. Something changed in his expression. When he spoke, his voice was softer. "I know you don't know anything about me, but there's nothing I wouldn't do for your brother, and that includes looking after you and making sure you have a secure place to stay. The house still needs a significant amount of work before it'll be safe. There are issues with the floors, the cabinets, the roof, the windows… You shouldn't be here by yourself when you don't know where the danger spots are. Sebastian bought the place because he knew he could count on me to help him do the renovations. I'm not backing out on my part of that deal."

Harley paused. He made a fair point about her not knowing how to navigate the current quirks of the house… but would it really be that difficult to learn? She was a good bit lighter than Garrett—it was possible that the same floorboards that might crack under his weight would hold hers just fine. And the prospect of unstable flooring seemed a lot less risky than welcoming a stranger into what was now her home. She'd had too many bad experiences to invite trouble like that.

Garrett gave every sign of being a good guy. But so had Thomas. He'd set himself up as her knight in shining armor early in their relationship, having her move in with him so he could take care of her. She'd soon learned that his real goal was getting her under his thumb. So many of her earlier experiences as she'd gone in and out of foster homes and group homes had been the same. Nothing that seemed good ever lasted. Kindness faded. If she was lucky, it just disappeared. Other times, it turned vicious.

But how to approach this situation with a man who was her brother's best friend and was grieving, too? His grief might even be stronger than hers, since Garrett had actually known Sebastian in recent years. It felt wrong to kick him out of a house that that had been his home as well as Sebastian's.

"I get that keeping your word is important to you, but I won't hold you to it. And…" She was just going to have to say it. "I'm not comfortable with you staying in the house. I'm sorry. I can tell that this place means a lot to you, and obviously Sebastian was happy to have you here—but you're still a stranger to me, and this isn't going to work."

He studied her for a long minute, and she wondered what he saw when his eyes strayed to her left cheek. Was he reading her face like it was a history of what she'd endured? She was afraid so. Another reason not to have him around. She didn't want to answer questions about her past, not to someone she didn't know.

"Let me at least show you the house before you decide. It's got some oddities you should be aware of, especially because of the construction." He gave her a warm smile that might have been charming if she weren't so wary. But she supposed she did need a tour of the place.

"All right," she agreed and opened her trunk. She had just one suit-case, a box, and her laptop bag.

"Is this it?" he asked as he reached for the suitcase and box.

"I travel light." She shouldered the laptop bag and tried to put the memory of sneaking out of Thomas's house behind her. She'd had to leave plenty of her things, but she couldn't regret that. Sacrificing material things was a small price to pay for escaping him. Besides, she no longer wanted to wear the clothing Thomas had picked out for her and insisted she wear. The garments were too flashy, too showy. Not at all to her taste. She hadn't minded leaving most of them behind. She took her laptop bag, closed her trunk, and followed Garrett up the steps to the porch.

"As you can see," he said, "I've replaced the bad floorboards on that end." The unpainted boards showed, standing out from the ones that were a well-worn slate gray. "I'm working my way to the other side, so if you walk down there, it might feel soft and springy. It's best to avoid stepping on those."

"I'll keep that in mind."

"I wouldn't recommend leaning on the railing, either. It all needs to be replaced, but it's low on the priority list. Oh, and the lock can be tough." He was at the door, where he inserted his key. "You've got to jiggle the key a bit until you feel it catch."

"Noted." She was starting to feel panicky. Three issues already, before they'd even gotten through the door. Just what had she gotten herself into?

"Here we are." He swung both doors open and stood to the side for her to enter. "The foyer's been redone, and I've mostly finished working on the stairs. They're solid—they just need some prettying up."

The steps to the second floor went up from just inside the front door. The foyer itself and a hall that ran past the stairs on the left looked beautiful. The floors were freshly varnished and shiny, the walls a creamy white. This was better than she'd expected, and it made her a little more hopeful.

"The formal living room is through here." He put her suitcase down and opened a set of pocket doors. The room they revealed was gutted down to the studs. A ladder, a work light, and tools were the only items inside, and those were scattered across a badly damaged wooden floor. Her heart sank again. "It doesn't look like much now, but it'll be a showstopper, I promise. Come see the den. It's through here." He crossed the room to another set of doors.

Okay, this was better. New drywall was up, and the woodwork looked to have been recently redone. The walls hadn't been painted yet, but it was far better than the other room.

"The Wi-Fi is out, but I can get that up and working quickly if you need it," he said.

"I work remotely, so I'll need internet access tomorrow." She had a morning meeting with the publisher she worked for that she didn't want to miss.

"I'll take care of it first thing in the morning." He led her through the rest of the downstairs, where the kitchen was under construction but usable, a formal dining room was in similar shape as the living room, and the powder room looked done. Garrett kept up a steady stream of chatter about the house and the plans for different parts of it. The cheerful cadence of his voice was so soothing that she almost felt comfortable by the time they returned to the foyer.

"You've got four bedrooms and two bathrooms upstairs. The work up there is also half-done. We fixed up the bedrooms we needed to live in." He picked up her suitcase, and she followed him up the stairs. "I've been using that room." He pointed to an open door on the left. "And Sebastian was over here in the main bedroom. I thought you'd…"

"Yes, that's fine." She walked to the doorway and looked in. The room had deep blue walls and the same dark woodwork found throughout the house. It was masculine without being overpowering. A framed picture sat on top of a dresser, drawing her attention. It was a snapshot of her and Sebastian when they were little, sitting together in a wagon.

She couldn't have been more than three and had no memory of the moment. She picked up the frame to study the image. Sebastian was behind her, and her head obscured half of his face. She squinted at the grainy picture. She'd been struggling since Sebastian first contacted her to remember what he'd looked like as a child. This picture helped, but only a little since it wasn't good quality.

"You and Sebastian?" Garrett was suddenly behind her. She sucked in a breath and whirled away. How had he gotten so close without her hearing? He was far too big a man to move that quietly. "Easy, now." He took a step back. "I didn't mean to spook you."

"I'm a little overwhelmed, that's all." Her heart was racing.

"I can give you a moment."

A moment wouldn't help. She needed Garrett out of her space. "It's fine. Thanks for the tour. I can see that there is a lot of work to be done yet, but I think it would be better if I hire a contractor. I need it finished quickly." She could see from his face that she was insulting him, which wasn't her intention. "Don't get me wrong. I appreciate what you've done, but I can't expect you to keep coming here to work every minute you're not on a mission."

"I made a commitment to Sebastian." Garrett's jaw had a stubborn set to it, and the large bedroom started to feel small. He was between her and the doorway, and she didn't like that. Taking a chance, she decided to be straight-up honest with him.

"I just got out of a… a bad relationship." An understatement, but he didn't need the details. "If I hire someone who does this professionally, they won't need to live here while they're doing the work. I'm not sure I'm ready to share a house with a man again."

He pressed his lips together, but he looked more concerned than hurt or angry. "I'm sorry for your situation. I can see how that would make things difficult for you. But I promise I'll keep on my side of the hallway and out of your way as much as possible. Please don't think I would ever disrespect you. Your brother was my closest friend." His voice cracked slightly on the words. "I made a commitment to him to fix up this house. The supplies are purchased. It's just the labor left. Let me finish what I started. Please."

She could see he felt he had to do this. And, she realized, she didn't have the money to pay someone else to do the work, with Sebastian's bank accounts tied up in probate. If Garrett didn't complete it, she'd be stuck living in a half-finished house for at least another month.

"Show me the rest of the house," she said, still uncertain which course to take. She steeled herself to walk toward him. He immediately stepped aside, letting her pass into the hall. That was in his favor. He understood to keep his distance—and to clear the path between her and an exit. "What's behind this door?" She reached for the knob and opened it.

"Attic entrance. It's a big space and could be usable with some work."

Determined to know the house that she now owned, she went up the narrow staircase and stepped onto wide-planked, unfinished floors.

Garrett was right. The attic was large, with a window facing in each direction to give it light. She walked toward the one that had a view of the lake.

"Wait." Strong arms came around her just as she realized her foot was hovering over empty space. He exhaled, his breath warm on her neck, and his voice rumbled in his chest, which was pressed to her back. "The floor doesn't extend the whole width of the attic."

She'd nearly stepped off into nothing. If he hadn't stopped her, she'd have been hurt—or worse. "Thank you," she whispered as he guided her back toward the stairs. His hold on her felt firm and safe, but she knew that had to be an illusion. There was no such thing as safety. Not that she'd ever found, anyway.

Her long-lost brother had said she could trust Garrett, but she hadn't even known Sebastian as an adult. In any case, trust had to be earned. She would never give it away freely again. As soon as Garrett released her, she rushed down the stairs away from him. In the hallway, she leaned against the wall, trying to calm her breathing.

"Harley, I'm sorry if I scared you." Garrett closed the attic door. "But I need to stay and make this house safe for you to live in. If something happened to you, I'd never forgive myself."

She understood where he was coming from, but she was still so uncertain about everything. She needed some time. "I'm exhausted. Let me sleep on it. Whatever I decide, I won't kick you out until you have a place to go." She didn't like the idea of sleeping with him in the house, even for a night or two, but she didn't see an alternative.

"Works for me. We can talk in the morning. For now, I'll be outside working on the porch if you need me." He disappeared down the stairs to the ground floor.

She moved to the window at the end of the hall and looked out. Her hand went automatically to her belly. "This is our home now, baby," she murmured, rubbing her hand over the barely perceptible bump. "And no matter what I have to do, I swear I'm going to make it safe for you." Whether that meant putting up with the unnervingly attractive Garrett Moore for a while longer, she still couldn't say.

3

———————

Garrett rose at six and worked out. By the time Harley was up, he was restoring the Wi-Fi in the den so she could get online. He was determined to do what he could to make her comfortable in her new home.

He got that it was a lot for her to take in. Finding and losing her brother and inheriting a half-renovated home were big changes, and she was going to need support. He wanted her to understand that he was there for her. She probably wasn't familiar with how SEALs operated, but by virtue of being Sebastian's sister, she was part of the SEAL family. That meant she had people in her corner, whether she knew what to do with them or not.

"Good morning," she said as she came into the den. "I thought I heard you in here."

"Hey," he replied. "I'm dealing with the electrical issue so we can reboot the Wi-Fi. You said you needed to work today."

"Thanks. I do." She opened her mouth as if to say more, but then didn't. Her eyes flicked to his, then away, clearly nervous. He was used to people being at ease with him. He'd always had a knack for developing rapport with people he met. He had tons of friends for just that reason. But Harley was proving very difficult to win over.

"No problem. This outlet is good to go." He pointed to the one near a desk. "You can plug your laptop into it. The modem is in the kitchen. I'm going to get it back online, so you should be in business in a few minutes. Can I get you some breakfast?"

"No, thanks. I'll grab something later."

His Idaho upbringing made him want to feed her. Food fixed problems in his family's household, and it appeared Harley had a host of problems to be fixed. But he forced himself not to push the issue—not yet, at least. Strain showed in her eyes, and she was still skittish around him.

One thing at a time, he reminded himself before going to deal with the Wi-Fi. He rebooted the network and checked that it was working before going outside to continue replacing porch floorboards. He'd only been out there for fifteen minutes when she came to the front door, her lips pursed.

"Sorry," she said, "but there was a pop, and the power went out in the den. Can you…" She gestured behind her.

He left what he was doing and followed her back into the house, where he immediately caught the scent of coffee. Before he even reached the den, he had an idea what the problem was. Sure enough, her laptop and a fancy-looking little coffee maker were plugged into the same outlet. He'd told her that outlet was usable, but he should have mentioned not to overload it.

"You tripped a breaker," he said, scrubbing a hand over his face. "The electricity in this room is dicey, and coffee makers pull a lot of juice when they're brewing."

"Oh… I'm sorry. I didn't know." She checked the time on her phone, looking nervous. "I guess I could go someplace else with internet access to get on my Zoom. Is there a library or a coffee shop with Wi-Fi nearby?"

"Sure, but I can have this fixed quickly. You don't need to go anywhere. You'll just need to make your coffee in the kitchen instead," he explained. Addressing the problem was a simple matter of resetting the breaker and reducing the electrical load.

"I can do that." She smiled then—a genuine smile, the first one he'd seen from her. It took his breath away. "I'm hooked on Nespresso," she said. "I'll be brewing individual cups all day, but I can walk to the kitchen to get them. Thanks. I… I feel like I'm causing more trouble for you."

"Don't worry about it." He went to the basement and reset the breaker, then returned to the den. She'd moved the coffee maker to the kitchen counter and was at the desk with her laptop open. She gave him a little wave, but her attention was focused on the screen, where she was listening to someone.

He returned to work on the porch until his stomach started to growl. Maybe he'd grab one of the bagels Mia had brought him from the bakery yesterday. He'd already had a protein shake, but that had been hours earlier. When he got to the kitchen, he found Harley standing by her coffee maker just as it finished another cup. It wasn't plain old black coffee like he drank. Hers had a frothy topping on it. She pulled the mug from the machine and took a sip.

"So you drink this all day?" he asked as he sliced a bagel and put it in the toaster oven. He took a chance and added another one.

"Oh yes. It's decaf, though, so I won't get all jittery on you."

"I wasn't worried about that." He could see there was plenty else to worry about in regard to her. He wanted to respect her privacy, but he couldn't ignore his protective streak. Since she wasn't heading back to the den with her mug, maybe she was giving him an opening to be friendly. He'd take it, because he didn't want her to be uncomfortable around him. He grabbed the cream cheese from the refrigerator. "Want a bagel?"

"Maybe a half." She sat at the small kitchen table with her mug clutched in her hands while he spread the cream cheese on the freshly toasted bagels. He put them on a plate and set it between them when he sat across from her.

"Work going okay?" he asked, figuring that was a nonthreatening way to open the conversation.

"Fine. The usual morning meeting. I have three projects in various stages, so I'll spend the rest of the day working on those." She'd told him the day before that she worked for an academic publisher who specialized in science textbooks. "I'm a little behind, but I'll get caught up soon. What are you working on?"

"The front porch, still. If I get back to it, I should be able to replace the rest of the floorboards before sundown and check one project off the list."

"It appears to be a long list." She picked up a bagel half and took a bite.

"Yeah. Sebastian and I took on a lot. Now that it's just me, I'm..." Everything had gone sideways when Sebastian was killed. The house project was going to be more difficult to handle alone, but he would get it done. On top of that, though, he was worried about how the mission had gone so badly wrong. Not that he was going to mention the mission to Harley. He couldn't do anything about that except support Jonathan, who was in the hot seat when it came to explaining what had gone wrong.

"It's all different. I'm sorry." She was sympathizing with him when it was her brother who was gone. "About yesterday," she continued, "I don't mean to be ungrateful for all you've done, but I just… I need more control over my own life right now. That's why I think it's best if you—"

"Hello?" a voice called from the front door. Patrick. "Anyone home?"

"In the kitchen," Garrett responded. He wanted to finish this conversation with Harley, to reiterate his commitment to complete the work. She didn't need to go to the inconvenience and expense of hiring someone else to do the labor on projects he could complete before he had to return to base.

"Hi there." Imogen walked into the room, followed by Patrick. Both of them held grocery bags in their arms. "We figured Garrett didn't have a whole lot of food. Not enough for two." She eyed the bagels. "Those are a start, but we brought a few more things. I'm Imogen, and this is my husband, Patrick. We're your neighbors." She gestured in the direction of their house.

Harley stood and shook hands with them. "Nice to meet you."

Garrett noted that Harley made eye contact with Imogen, who was one of the kindest people Garrett knew, but barely glanced at Patrick.

"I'm sorry about your brother," Patrick said. "He was one of the best men I've ever known. I mean that. He'd do anything for anybody. He even watched our kids for us one evening on zero notice when our sitter fell through and we had a wedding to go to. Our son was a baby, and he slept through it, but our daughter is a handful sometimes." Patrick grinned. He might say that about Ellery, but his third-grade daughter was the joy of his life.

"Where are the kids?" Garrett asked.

"On a playdate. We're headed to pick them up but wanted to stop in and say hello first," Imogen explained. "We are truly sorry about Sebastian. Words can't express what he meant to all of us."

"Thanks. I wish I'd known him as an adult," Harley said, her voice quiet.

Warm-hearted Imogen gave Harley a hug. "We all wish he was still here with us. You sit down and finish your bagel while I put these groceries away. Then Patrick and I will get out of your hair."

Garrett helped unpack the bags, grateful that his friends had thought to stop by with food. Harley had needed a boost. She had grit—he could see that—but he wanted things to be easier for her. Patrick and Imogen's visit seemed to help. He saw Harley smiling as she waved goodbye to them from the porch.

The sunshine brought out the caramel-colored highlights in her dark hair, and he was once again struck by how pretty she was. He felt a tug of attraction and ignored it. They were both dealing with enough. Besides, she was his friend's sister. In bro code, that meant she was off-limits. And in any case, right now she needed his friendship more than anything.

And his help. Before their visitors arrived, she'd been about to say something about him leaving. So he'd prepared a logical argument for why he should stay.

"Harley, we need to lay out a plan for what has to get done before I'm due back on base."

"I—"

"Just let me list off the most important projects," he said quickly. "There are things that can't wait. First, there's the electrical issues, as you saw this morning. Then, I want to finish the walls and woodwork in the living room and formal dining room. I might not get the rooms painted, but I can do the heavy lifting on those projects. A couple of the windows have issues, and I want to replace the locks on the exterior doors."

Maybe add a security system as well. He and Sebastian hadn't gotten around to that yet, but Garrett didn't want her living there alone without at least a doorbell camera.

"I'd like to get the landscaping started, too. Some of the shrubs have seen better days, and a few of the trees need to be trimmed. Now, down at the boathouse—"

"Garrett, you can't possibly get all that done," she said. She paused, looking as startled as he was that she'd interrupted him, but soldiered on. "So I'd like you to prioritize and only do what's necessary for the house to be livable in the time that you have."

He hesitated, processing her words. It seemed she was letting him stay, but he wanted to be clear. "In the kitchen, I thought you were getting ready to tell me to bug out."

"I was," she admitted, "but... I might have been wrong about that." She brushed a curl back over her shoulder. "I'd like you to stay and finish what you can. I know you won't get everything done." She glanced to where his workstation was set up at the end of the porch. "Once I get access to Sebastian's accounts, I'll hire someone to do the rest. I want to be clear that I don't expect you to come back between missions to do more work."

Fair enough. "That works for me," he agreed. He didn't love the idea of her having to pay for work he'd gladly do for free, but he appreciated that she wouldn't want to wait for him to come by and handle projects in fits and starts. It wasn't like he was going to be able to stick around. This wasn't his town. Once he'd done what Harley would let him do, he'd move on.

"Good." Her phone rang, and she pulled it from her pocket, tapping the screen to answer it.

"You bitch," a man's voice snarled, audible even at a distance. "Don't think you can just walk away from me, Harley. I'll find you, and when I do, I'm going to make you hurt. I'm going to—"

Harley hung up. Her hands were visibly shaking as she put her phone away.

"Who was that?" Garrett demanded. Instinct had him scanning the area around them for signs of danger, even though the man had made it clear he didn't know where she was.

She sighed. "My soon-to-be ex-husband."

Husband? Sebastian had said she was in a relationship, but Garrett hadn't expected her to be married. She wore no ring. But then, why would she wear the ring of a guy like that?

"He doesn't know where I am, so it's okay."

"It's not okay that anyone talks to you like that, ever. Has he hurt you before?" Garrett asked, but he knew the answer. The bruise near her temple proved that. "He has, hasn't he."

"It's not your problem." She stood up straight and squared her shoulders.

"Have you filed for divorce? Gotten a restraining order against him?" Legal measures were far from guaranteed protection, but they were the first steps in officially separating her from what was clearly an abusive relationship.

"Not yet, but I will soon." Her chin was up, and he was reminded that she was tougher than she looked.

"It's not safe for you to be alone." That was undeniable. A security system was a must, but that didn't feel like enough. He couldn't unhear the threat against her—nor would he if he could. "I'm sticking around until I'm sure you're settled in and safe from *him*."

"He doesn't know where I am," she repeated.

"It's not that hard to locate people. I want you to have backup if he shows his face here. And you need to do whatever you can to make sure the law is on your side." Garrett waited, giving her time to process what he'd said. He'd camp out on the lawn if she wanted him out of the house, but he would make sure she was safe. He owed Sebastian that, and he felt that he owed her—though he couldn't explain why. It could be his bond with Sebastian, but there was something about her, about the way her brown eyes met his, about the way she looked fragile on the surface but was tough at the core.

Whatever it was, he wasn't going anywhere.

"I suppose you're right," she finally said. "If he finds me… I do need protection." It must have cost her to admit that, but he was glad she did.

"I'll be here for you." It was a pledge he could make, at least for now.

4

Harley checked her phone, dreading any new messages from Thomas. She'd blocked his number, but he was too clever to be stopped by that. He wouldn't call from a number she recognized. That was why she'd answered the phone on the porch a few days earlier, inadvertently exposing one of her secrets.

She was carefully keeping another from Garrett. He didn't need to know she was pregnant. It was too early for her to be showing, although it wouldn't be long. She was past the three-month mark. Hopefully, by the time a noticeable baby bump appeared, Garrett would be back on his base and her divorce would be in progress. Until then, she'd be walking on eggshells, constantly checking over her shoulder. Simply thinking about Thomas made her anxious.

She took a deep breath, practicing the circle breathing technique to calm herself. Getting upset wasn't good for the baby. She needed to focus on other things, like her work and making decisions about the house renovations.

She needed to do something about this pantry, for instance. She studied the small space off the kitchen. It had shelves, but it was barely wide enough for her to slip in sideways. That would never do if she was raising a child. She'd need more storage.

"Are you having another idea?" Garrett asked as he came into the kitchen and headed to the refrigerator for a bottle of water.

"Maybe." They'd gone through the plans that Sebastian had made for the house and sorted out what Garrett could accomplish before his leave was up. She'd had some suggestions for alterations, like for the small room off the main bedroom that appeared to have no purpose. He had thought it would make a great walk-in closet, but she saw it differently and asked him to just finish repairing the plaster walls. To her, it was the perfect space for a nursery. It had a window that faced south and got plenty of sunlight, and it was just big enough for a crib, dresser, and rocker. She could see it painted a sage green and decorated in a woodsy theme. She'd take care of the cosmetic touches after he left.

"Looking for more storage?" Garrett asked, bringing her attention back to the kitchen pantry area.

"Yes. Do you think it's possible to remove the bar?" Next to the pantry was a counter with space below for wine storage and a rack above to hang stemmed glasses. "If we took that out, could this area be used differently?" She indicated how she wanted it to be open to the kitchen.

"Should be doable." He knocked on the wall that separated the areas. "I don't see why there would be any pipes in the wall, so it'd be an easy demo. The home improvement store has some great organizers for kitchen storage. I could install them and put in accordion doors so it could be hidden. Like so."

He reached around her, indicating where the doors would go. His chest bumped against her arm, making her look up. His face was so close. She saw a fleeting look in his green eyes, a look that said he was attracted to her. Did he want to kiss her? Her face heated. Did she want him to?

If their circumstances were different, if she'd met him at some other time—yes.

But not now. She was too unsettled. That was the story of her life. She'd get into what seemed like a good situation, only to have it fall apart. Foster homes, group homes, apartments, and then Thomas. Too often, she'd gotten attached even though she knew better.

She took a step back. It wasn't smart to even be having these thoughts around Garrett. He'd been kind and sweet, and he was damn sexy with a tool belt slung around his narrow hips, but… no.

"This must be hard for you," she said, to bring herself back to why she was temporarily sharing a home with this man. "You and Sebastian made plans, and now…"

"I miss him every day." Garrett's tone was blunt. "But this was never my house. He made the choices, just as you are now. This is your home, and I want you to be happy in it." She'd given up believing people, especially men, but she was tempted to believe him. "If my plan for the pantry sounds good, come see what I've accomplished in the living room."

For a second, she thought he'd take her hand. Instead, he gestured for her to walk in front of him to the formal living room. She pushed open the pocket doors, and a blast of varnish fumes made her gag. She turned quickly to escape the smell and ran straight into Garrett's muscled chest.

"Got to get outside." She pushed against him and stumbled toward the front door. His arm came around her waist, and he guided her out into the fresh air. Seconds later, she was sitting on the top porch step with her head between her knees, Garrett's large hand rubbing circles on her back as she fought the urge to vomit. She hadn't experienced any morning sickness so far, but that smell had triggered something awful.

"Do you need water? A doctor?" His voice was calm, but she heard an edge of nerves in it. She shook her head and squeezed her eyes closed. Slowly, the nausea receded, and she could focus on the feel of his hand, the slight breeze, the sounds of birds chirping in the nearby magnolia tree.

"I'm okay now," she said, lifting her head. "The smell got me."

"That's an… unusual reaction. Are you always so sensitive to chemicals?"

"No." She was still reluctant to tell him about her pregnancy, but maybe someone in Hartsville should know, in case there was a problem. And she *was* starting to trust Garrett. He was a… friend, and Sebastian had trusted him, so it felt safe. As safe as anything could. "I'm pregnant."

"Whoa! What?" He drew his hand back in shock. "God, Harley, you should have told me."

"Why? I mean, it doesn't change anything about our arrangement." He was leaving in less than three weeks to return to base, and he had no responsibility to her past that.

"It absolutely does. I was hoping to see you settled before I left, but there's no way the house will be ready for a baby by then, and what if there are delays in finding a contractor? Not to mention you living here while work is going on, if you're having difficulties with smells." His expression was still stark surprise. "When will the baby be here?"

"I'm at fourteen weeks, so that's just into the second trimester. Pregnancies are forty weeks."

"I'm aware. I've got twelve nieces and nephews back in Idaho."

It was her turn to be shocked. "Twelve? How many siblings do you have?" She was imagining a huge family and wondering what that would be like.

"Three older sisters. I'm familiar with babies and kids. God, I wish you'd told me about the baby right away. I could have prioritized things differently."

She shrugged. The baby wasn't anyone's business but hers. Long ago, she'd learned to keep her personal information to herself. The more people knew, the more they could use against her.

And the one time she'd violated her own policy, she'd paid. She was still paying. She'd moved in with Thomas and married him quickly because she'd trusted him—and because she'd been desperate. She'd lost her job at the publishing house she'd worked at since high school when they downsized to move half of their operation overseas. Between rent and car payments, her savings had gone fast. Thomas had seemed like the answer to her prayers, so she'd leaped before she looked for the first time in her life.

And where that had gotten her? Pregnant. Alone. Living in fear.

But she did have this house, which was more than she'd ever expected. Despite its current condition, it was substantial and would be beautiful. It might be too large for just her and a child, and she supposed the wise thing to do after it was renovated might be to sell it or rent it out, but she'd see about that later. She had so many decisions to make.

If only she had her brother. The ache of never truly knowing him nagged at her. If only…

"You can't go through a pregnancy without some support," Garrett declared. He was no longer touching her, but he'd stayed on the step with her.

"Of course I can. Women do all the time." She needed to find a doctor in the area, but she had plenty of time to prepare for the birth and bringing the baby home. It wasn't going to be easy, but not much in her life had been. She'd make it work. It wouldn't be the first time that she'd faced a tough situation on her own.

"Sebastian wouldn't want you to." Garrett's voice had softened.

"You're not Sebastian. And you're not responsible for me," she said, because it seemed Garrett needed to hear it. "You don't owe me anything, understand?" She didn't know him well, but he struck her as the type to shoulder burdens that weren't his. She appreciated his gallantry, but she didn't need him. If he finished what he planned to on the house, that would be enough.

"Does your husband know about the baby?" Garrett asked.

She shook her head and was about to explain that it was better that way when her phone pinged with a message. She pulled it out, glancing at the home screen. The number wasn't in her contacts, but it was Thomas. The charming, persuasive side of his personality. It was as if he knew she was thinking of him at that moment.

"Come on, baby," the message read. "Give us another chance. Miss you. Love you."

She pressed the button to make the screen go dark, but the message still made her shiver. Her stomach, which had finally settled, began to quake again. Thomas had never loved her, and he certainly didn't now. It was simply part of his routine: if she didn't respond to threats, he'd try a different tactic. It had been the same in person. He'd be super sweet and loving for days, sometimes even weeks, after beating her. Just long enough that she'd begin to think he was truly sorry and that he cared about her.

Then, when she started to feel safe again, he'd come home from work angry and take it out on her. She'd wanted to get away from him for months, but she'd been trapped. When they'd gotten married, she'd made the mistake of opening a joint account with him. She didn't realize right away that he was withdrawing her entire paycheck every week, leaving her with no money to call her own. When she asked him about it, he became belligerent and threatening. Without money or family, she'd seen no way to escape him until Sebastian had contacted her.

Even though her brother was gone, he'd given her the means to leave Thomas. She was free. She had to tell herself that, because she kept waking in the night terrified about what Thomas would do to her and their baby if he figured out where she was.

"If he finds you, I'll make sure you're safe," Garrett said, as if he needed to speak the words. He must have read the message, too. Part of her was glad he was there and knew about the baby and Thomas. Still, she couldn't get into the habit of relying on him. She already was, too much, with the house and now this.

"I can take care of myself." She hadn't always done a great job of that, but she had to now. Her baby deserved better.

"I *will* protect you and your child," Garrett insisted, and she decided not to argue with him.

She stood, feeling steadier, and he rose with her, hovering without touching her. "Thank you."

When she got into the house, she went to her bedroom, needing some time to herself. A window was open, and she stood near it for a minute, looking out toward the lake and enjoying the fresh air. This would be a good place to raise her son or daughter. She rubbed her hand over her stomach, something she'd been careful to avoid doing in front of Garrett. Now that he knew about the baby, she wouldn't have to be so cautious.

Despite what she'd said to him outside, she was glad he was with her.

5

Garrett whacked the wall in the kitchen with a crowbar, beginning the renovation on the pantry. The old plaster had to come down, which was always messy—but satisfying, too. And a little destruction was just what he needed, since he was still reeling from Harley's announcement the day before.

She was pregnant. He'd been concerned for her before, but now his worry had increased tenfold. How was he going to go on a mission knowing that her husband was threatening her and also was a danger to her child? He didn't have his orders yet for his next deployment, but SEAL missions tended to be long. He might not make it back before the baby was born.

And what the hell was she supposed to do by herself in this big, unfinished house?

He hit the wall again and peeled back a large section, revealing the studs but thankfully no pipes or electrical conduits. He kept at it, his body working as quickly as his mind. He'd made choices when he'd become a SEAL. He'd chosen to limit his love life to quick flings, the kind where both parties walked away and no one got hurt because neither expected more. Being a SEAL came first for him. He'd been happy with that, knowing it was for the best if he didn't have attachments at home to worry about when he was deployed.

He had no idea how his buddies with wives did it. Kenton, Anderson, and Patrick insisted that having a family was worth the struggle, but Garrett couldn't see it. He wasn't even involved with Harley, not really, but he was twisted up about how to help her. He wanted to do Sebastian proud by ensuring that she was okay. Better than okay. She needed to be healthy and safe, and so did her baby. How was he supposed to balance that with doing his job?

He smashed his crowbar into the wall again, and plaster crumbled at his feet, sending up a plume of dust.

"That's quite a hole." Harley must have come in while he was working. "I…"

"Step back," he said, not wanting her to breathe in the dust. He checked the area around where he was working. Old plaster could be unpredictable. Cracks splintered off in all directions. It wouldn't take much for more of the wall to come down.

"I guess you're really opening up some space. That's great," she said from near the kitchen table, which he'd draped in plastic.

"The pantry will be even bigger than you wanted, I guess." The dust was still sifting down, but he studied the opening. Something wasn't quite right about it. Old houses had peculiarities. There was no doubt about that. He and Sebastian had found an ironing board inside a wall in one of the bedrooms when they were doing demo upstairs. Old newspapers had been tucked under floorboards, and they'd discovered toy soldiers by the dozen buried in one of the flower beds. Some kid must have had quite the battle scene going on.

"Plenty of room for baby food and kid snacks," she said.

"True enough." His sisters' kitchens seemed to overflow with cookies and crackers, since his nieces and nephews never stopped eating. But this hole revealed an opening that went deeper than he'd expected. Maybe he should ask Patrick to come over and give his opinion.

"I'm really happy you made time to do this project." Something about her voice was off. He turned to where she stood. Her knuckles were white where she was gripping the top of a kitchen chair. Was she worried about the demo? Or…

Her face grew paler, and he reached her in four long steps. "You need to sit." He pulled out a chair and then knelt in front of her. She didn't look good. He might not have thought anything of it if he didn't know she was pregnant. His sisters would kick his ass if he suggested that a pregnant woman was some delicate flower, but babies could drain a lot of the mother's resources so they'd have the fuel to grow, which could leave the woman feeling run-down. Plus, he didn't like the dark smudges under her eyes. She must not have slept well the night before, which was no surprise when he considered the stress she was under.

As if on cue, her phone screen glowed with a message. He didn't read it, but he had seen yesterday's and got the jackass's game. He'd seen guys before who could range from loving to abusive in a second.

"Thomas?" he asked gently.

"He left a voicemail earlier, too," she admitted, and if her skin could lose any more color, it did.

"Was he calling you names or trying to woo you?" It was really none of Garrett's business, but he hated that Thomas was putting her through this. Given the opportunity, he'd make sure the creep never bothered her again.

"Doesn't matter," she said with a shrug. She gave him a smile, but it was weak and tinged with exhaustion.

"Come on." In one motion, he rose to his feet and scooped her off the chair and into his arms. She needed a nap and didn't look like she had the energy to climb the stairs on her own.

"Put me down," she insisted halfheartedly as he headed for the stairs.

"Nope. You look tired enough to fall down, and I can't have that on my watch. It's nap time."

"I don't nap," she said, even as she snuggled against him with a yawn.

"Pregnant women nap, or so I've been told." His second oldest sister claimed that she'd slept through two of her pregnancies.

"Your sisters?" she asked.

"Yep."

"Twelve kids between them," she murmured. "They must be something."

"Intimidating is what they are," he confirmed as he carried her into her bedroom and lay her down. He covered her with a blanket that had been folded up at the foot of the bed. Then, even though he knew he should go, he sat next to her. He could excuse his behavior as just making sure she was comfortable, but he couldn't resist stroking her cheek for a moment. Her skin was soft and smooth, and he realized he wanted to stay with her until she slept.

But he had no right to do that, so he stood, putting some distance between them. "I'm going to the home improvement store." He needed to pick up a few supplies. "Anything I can get you while I'm out?"

"I don't think so. Thanks," she murmured, her eyes half-closed.

"I'd better find you right here when I come back." He let himself touch her cheek one last time before he left, but she was already asleep.

He was gone just an hour, not wanting to leave her alone any longer than necessary. When he checked on her, she was sitting up in bed, reading a book. She looked better. Not entirely rested, but better.

"Hi," she said, putting her book on the nightstand.

"Hey." He came closer, clutching a bag from the store. "I picked up some things for you while I was out."

"Oh? Like what?"

"Ginger chews." He handed her a package. He'd had to make an extra stop at a drug store for those. "My sisters swear by them to help with morning sickness."

"Good to know." She took them. "That was very thoughtful of you."

"No problem, and I got some home design magazines, too," he said. "One is about nurseries and kid spaces, and the other is for family homes. It had some good ideas for storage in a mudroom." He'd flipped through several at the store until he'd found ones he thought she'd like.

She smiled as she took the magazines from him. "I didn't expect…"

"If you like, you can mark pages of stuff you think you want, and I'll see what I can do." His time here was going to run out, but he couldn't seem to stop himself from trying to help her. "You never know, you might see the perfect thing for this house."

"I'll do that tonight." She held the magazines and studied him. She met his eyes more often than in the first days, but he still wasn't sure how she saw him.

"Good. I'm going to go back to work in the kitchen. I need to get the rest of that wall down and see what we've got."

"I'll help." She tossed back the blanket and put her feet on the floor.

He wanted to tell her to stay away from the dust and mess, but this was her house. He would just make sure she did it carefully. "If you like."

Back in the kitchen, he insisted she don safety goggles and gloves before she picked up the crowbar and took a swing at the wall near the hole. Another large crack formed, splintering off in every direction.

"It's coming down," she said, sounding excited. She took aim at the wall a second time, hitting it with a solid thump. Plaster broke loose and cascaded down. Garrett reached for her, pulling her back to a safe distance as more plaster fell to the floor.

He could have let her go, but he didn't, and she made no move to step away from him, either. He liked having her in his arms. He wasn't going to overthink that.

What he did have to do was deal with the wreckage. When the plaster stopped falling and the dust thinned, they moved closer. He'd thought something wasn't right about this area of the house. There was a small window on the exterior that he hadn't been able to account for inside, but he hadn't expected this.

A small room, maybe five by seven feet, had been walled off. It had a vaulted ceiling, giving it a fancy feel. What had this room been? Why had it been sealed away? And how on earth was he going to deal with it on his limited schedule?

"Well, damn," he muttered. "That's gonna change things." His plans for the pantry were completely blown now. He was going to have to work double time to deal with this. "Careful." He kept his arm around her waist as she tried to move closer to the mess. "I need to clean this up. I don't want you to get hurt."

"I want to see what's in there." She nudged forward.

"That's not wise until I make sure it's secure."

She turned her head and smiled up at him. "Relax. It's a surprise, not a tragedy. A fun surprise, too. How often do you discover a secret room? Way cool."

"It's a setback for your plans." His plans, too. And he'd already restructured those too many times to suit him.

"Maybe, but it's nice to have an exciting setback for a change," she said, reminding him that her life hadn't exactly been full of good surprises.

So maybe she was right, and this was a happy accident. He tried to see it from her perspective.

"They walled over the doorway and everything. Weird." She pointed to a door that someone had nailed studs over to create the wall. "Can it be salvaged?"

He looked more closely. "Probably." He pulled a few remaining pieces of plaster down and stepped between the studs. She was right on his heels, ready to explore. "Watch your step." He took her hand as they moved farther into the room. He pushed aside the ancient curtains on the window, letting more light in. One wall was lined with a set of shelves, along with a kid-sized table and chairs.

"It was a playroom," she gasped, dropping his hand to rush to the shelves. "Someone just left it all in here and closed it off. Why? Oh, my. Look at this old Monopoly game… and a tea set." Her voice changed on the last words as she pulled a basket from the shelf. She took it to the table and removed a tiny blue teapot with matching cups and saucers. "I never had…"

She fell silent as she began arranging the tea set on the small table as if she were hosting a party. He understood what she hadn't said. She'd never had a tea set as a kid. That wasn't something he'd have thought of as important, but it clearly meant something to her.

"Join me?" she asked, taking a seat in one of the chairs. He eyed the other one. Kid furniture wasn't going to hold him, especially a chair that was several decades old. But he didn't want to disappoint her, so he moved the chair and knelt on the floor beside the table.

"Will this do?"

"Just fine. Tea?" She poured imaginary tea into his cup and pretended to add sugar. When she'd done the same for herself, she held her cup up to his in a toast. "To happy accidents."

"You're kind of amazing," he said.

She laughed. "I'm used to making lemonade out of life's lemons, that's all. I pride myself on that." She put her cup down on the saucer and looked around her. "I've come to expect bad things, so when a surprise turns out to be good, it's cause to celebrate. All in all, I'd say it's been a good day. Thank you for that."

"Me? What did I do?"

"Made me take a nap that I really needed, knocked a wall down in my house and revealed a secret room, and brought me candies and magazines. And the day's not even over yet."

"Anyone would have seen that you needed to rest, and the magazines weren't a big deal."

She raised her cup to her lips and took a pretend sip before speaking. "They were to me. I've received very few gifts in my life."

That hit him in the gut. He had a great family, and he was damn lucky. He didn't remember that often enough. "Harley, I'm sorry."

She waved him off. "Thomas gave me presents, but they were always as apologies. Apologies that he didn't mean." She didn't say what Thomas had to apologize for. Garrett could guess: he'd beat her up and then feel bad and buy a gift. She might even forgive him and think it was the last time, but then it would happen again. It was a textbook pattern of abuse, and she was damaged by it—but she was far from broken.

"This is nice," she said a minute later. "You're nice."

"Because I came to your tea party?" He really hadn't done anything special for her.

"Yes. I've always wanted to host one." She ran her hand along the edge of the old table. "I'd see it in kids' movies and think that's what happiness was."

"You'll have plenty of tea parties with your child." He might even be able to fix up this table and chairs. They were old pieces, but they could be made sturdy enough for her and a kid.

"I will," she said. "Now, that is a happy thought."

"And who knows? When the house is done, maybe you can host a tea party for adults." The lawn behind the house that led down to the boat dock would be the perfect place for an outdoor celebration.

Her eyes brightened. "I like that idea. Not that I know many people in Hartsville to invite."

"You'll meet them, and they'll be honored to come." He found himself leaning toward her over the small table.

"How about you? Will you come?" she asked, shifting closer to him.

"If I can." He couldn't make guarantees about where he would be down the road, but if he was stateside, he'd be here.

"I'm going to take that as a promise, whether you meant it to be one or not." She touched her fingertips to his cheek, her eyes meeting his.

There were dozens of reasons why he shouldn't kiss her, but in that moment, none of them were strong enough to stop him. He pressed his lips to hers, intending to keep it short and sweet. When her breath hitched and her lips parted, though, he deepened the kiss, enjoying the slow slide of her tongue against his. He cupped the back of her neck, feeling the silkiness of her hair against his hand. He could have stayed like that forever, but she drew back after a moment.

Her cheeks were rosy, her eyes unfocused. Then she blinked, and a giggle escaped her. It was the first such sound he'd heard from her. It made her seem younger, like life hadn't been so rough for her.

"That was unexpected," she whispered.

"Was it?" The kiss had felt right. Almost inevitable. But how could that be? He wasn't going to be sticking around. Nothing could or should happen here. "I should get back to work and clean this mess up." He rocked back on his heels.

"I'll help," she offered.

He shook his head. She didn't need to breathe in any more of the dust. "I've got it." He stood and pulled her to her feet. "Go out on the front porch and get some sunshine and fresh air." He gave her hand one last squeeze before turning away.

6

G arrett slid the veggie omelet onto a plate and put it on the table in front of Harley.

She looked up from the design magazine she was perusing. "You don't have to do that," she said with a smile. "I can make my own breakfast."

"My culinary skills are limited, so let me show off where I can." He'd eaten an hour earlier, after working out, but he wanted to make sure that she didn't just drink coffee for breakfast. Her fatigue from the day before concerned him, though she hadn't mentioned having morning sickness since her reaction to the smell of the varnish. He took that, at least, as a good sign and sat across from her with his coffee mug.

Things had been surprisingly easy between them since that kiss the day before. He'd gone back to work cleaning up the demo, while she'd dusted herself off and taken her laptop to the porch to work. They'd eaten dinner together and even walked down to the lake in the evening. They hadn't kissed again, which was just as well, he supposed, but they were… comfortable together. That pleased him. He didn't want to be a source of stress for her.

The constant calls she received from Thomas were doing a number on her. Her phone had rung several times the evening before, while they were walking. She hadn't answered, but he'd seen her body tense each time.

"What's your project for today?" she asked after eating a few forkfuls of omelet.

"That." He gestured toward the hole in the kitchen that led to the playroom. "I've been working on a plan—"

Her phone screen flashed with an incoming call. Instead of answering, she flipped the phone over.

"Thomas again?" Garrett asked.

"Who else?" she muttered. "That's five calls in the past hour. I keep letting them go to voicemail."

"Did you listen to any of the ones you got last evening?" He didn't want her to, since it was hard on her, but he also wanted to keep tabs on Thomas. If the asshole figured out where she was, he might let that slip in the messages. Then Garrett would know to be even more on his guard.

"Some," she admitted. "It's always the same. He alternates between threatening me and begging me to come back with all sorts of sweet talk and false promises. I'm not foolish enough to fall for that."

"I'm so sorry." Garrett felt compelled to apologize for the jerk, though the only thing they had in common was a Y chromosome.

"I'll survive," she said with a sigh. "I'm looking on the bright side. It feels good every time I delete one of those awful messages."

He could understand that. Still… "Are you saving them anywhere?"

"I've been transferring them to a file on my computer. I never want to hear them again, but before I left Florida, I spoke to a lawyer on one of those help lines who advised me to keep any evidence of harassment." Her phone pinged with a text message. Indecision crossed her face before she reached for the phone. "It might be someone from work." She turned the phone over and scowled at it. "Nope, Thomas."

All right, enough was enough.

"You need to take action," Garrett said, struggling to keep his voice even. He wanted her to get the divorce and restraining order rolling, but it wasn't up to him. He had to respect that those were her choices to make, even though he was itching to move forward. The longer she stalled, the worse the situation might become.

"I know. It's just..." She looked away.

"What, Harley?" He softened his tone.

She squeezed her eyes shut for a second. "Thomas is awful, and I will divorce him, but... it still hurts to give up on something that I thought would be good. I never had anyone special in my life, not since going into the foster system, and I wanted that connection. I just chose the wrong man."

She must have loved Thomas when she married him. For some reason, that bothered Garrett, but he understood where she was coming from. Getting married must have seemed like a dream come true—a way to not be alone in the world anymore. "You'll have the baby," he reminded her.

"Yeah, I will. My own little family." A glimmer of a tear showed in her eye, but she blinked it away. "That's a happy thought." She'd barely gotten the words out when her phone dinged with another message.

"I understand it's hard to let go of what you hoped that relationship would be," Garrett said. "But you don't deserve this harassment.

Don't you think it's time to talk to an attorney and get the divorce papers filed?"

She sighed. "Do you think Anthony Burke handles divorces?"

The lawyer handling Sebastian's will had seemed kind and sympathetic. And working with someone she'd already met might help her get over the hurdle of starting this process. "Let's call him and ask."

She'd eaten about half the omelet and was now toying with the rest. Garrett couldn't blame her for having lost her appetite. He couldn't imagine what she was feeling at the prospect of all she'd have to do in order to unload Thomas permanently.

Her focus was on her plate when she spoke again. "I just want to be safe from him and raise my baby to always feel loved and secure. That's not too much to ask, is it?"

"Not at all. You deserve that, and so does your baby. And you've got a beautiful place to do it." He shot a glance at the enormous hole in the wall and added, "Mostly beautiful."

She smiled. "It's messy, but discovering that secret room made my day."

He'd liked that part himself—and the kiss that followed even more. He couldn't expect it to be repeated, but he did want to help her feel better. "Hey, I've got an idea. Why don't we go to the garden center and see what they have? You said something about getting flowers for the front of the house."

"I'd like that." Her face brightened. "I have my morning Zoom in a few minutes. Can we go after that?"

"Sure. I'll work on the kitchen until you're ready to go." After she went into the den, he cleaned up from breakfast and got to work. He had to agree with her: the secret room was an unexpected bonus, even though it meant he had to completely rethink his plans for the pantry.

By the time she was done with her Zoom, he'd finalized a new sketch and removed the walled-over door, setting it aside to use later.

"Ready?" she asked. She had on sneakers with leggings and a bright pink sweater and looked adorable. Could he tell her that? It was on the tip of his tongue, but he thought better of it. "Just let me wash off the dust," he said instead.

After a call to Burke's office to arrange an appointment for the next day, they set out for the Mountain Vista Garden Center. Since it was early spring, most of the plants were still in the greenhouses, but the center's outdoor area was dotted with hardier shrubs and young trees.

"Oh, look at this." Harley rushed toward a perfectly shaped blue spruce that stood about six feet tall. "It reminds me of Christmas. I'd like one of those. Not today, but sometime." She moved on and fingered a juniper. "This is lovely, too. There are so many choices. When it's time for serious landscaping, how am I going to decide?"

"You have some decent shrubs around the house already, but others are old and need to be replaced. You might want to hire a designer from the center to help you make a plan." Garrett wouldn't be around at that point, since any serious work would have to wait until she had access to Sebastian's accounts, but he enjoyed watching her dream a little. She hadn't had much opportunity to do that in her life.

She continued to wander through the young trees, stopping to read tags, and even took pictures of a few that appealed to her.

"Okay. I'm ready to look at flowers," she said several minutes later.

"This way." Garrett had been here once with Patrick and Imogen, so he knew that the retail greenhouses were extensive and shoppers were allowed to browse through them. Once inside, he grabbed a cart. "I'm willing to walk up and down every aisle so you get a good idea of what they have."

"Seriously?" she asked. "That's nice of you."

He hoped he'd been nice about a lot of things with her. But she was unused to kindness from people, especially men, he supposed.

"Let's start with the annuals." He headed toward the rows of flowers that were just starting to bud. She walked close beside him, occasionally bumping into him as they moved. Almost like they were a couple, which he enjoyed. He liked seeing her show enthusiasm, too. That had been coming out more over the past week. She retreated to cautiousness at times, but he was seeing more of her personality.

"That's pretty." She pointed to one yellow bloom in a flat of plants that were still green.

"Snapdragon," he said. "They need lots of sun, but they're hardy."

"And you know this because…?" She tilted her head to the side and studied him.

"My mom loves flowers," he said with a shrug. "I helped her put in several new flower beds when I was a kid. For hours of hauling dirt and working the soil, she paid me in cookies."

"And hugs, I bet."

"Yeah. Those, too." He had no complaints about his childhood. If anything, it had been too idyllic. The only thing he'd missed out on was a brother, but he'd found brotherhood in the SEALs, especially with Sebastian. A wave of grief and guilt came with that thought. He didn't want to go there. Not when he was trying to bring some sunshine to Harley's life. "Those are cleome." He indicated the plants on the other side of the aisle. "They grow to about four feet tall and become uncontrollable. They're also self-seeders. Once you plant them, they'll keep coming back every year."

"Is that a bad thing?" She wrinkled her brow and studied the little plants.

"Can be." He remembered the pink and white blooms springing in every direction. "Mom tried for formal gardens one year, but the cleome destroyed that vision. They don't stay in neat rows."

"What did she do?" Harley was standing close to him again, her hands next to his on the cart.

"She went with it and claimed it was an English country-style garden instead."

"Wise of her. I have no idea what kind of garden I want or what flowers to plant. I've never had an opportunity. Well… just the one time."

"A foster home?" He wanted to know more about her.

"Yeah, it was really nice. Maude and Jim." Her expression turned wistful, and he thought she'd clam up, but as they started walking again, she surprised him by continuing. "I hadn't been in the system long when I went to live with them. Just a few temporary places, and at that point, kids always believe that the perfect family is just waiting for them." She stopped to look at the delicate blossom of a purple pansy.

He wanted to ask when that belief ended for her, but he didn't want to interrupt while she was in a sharing mood.

"They were great. Both had recently retired. Jim had been in the Navy, I think, and Maude was a librarian. She had so many books. I loved it. They'd never had kids of their own and wanted to foster in their retirement. I had my own room and toys that were just mine. And there was a big backyard. Maude let me help her bake cookies, and Jim taught me to throw a ball overhand."

"How long were you with them?" It sounded like a great place for a child struggling with her mother's death and the pain of being separated from her brother.

"Four or five months, I think. It was during the summer and fall. I remember the school was nice, and I felt like the other kids, since I had parents who… cared about me. Then Maude had a heart attack, and everything changed. Jim couldn't take care of a kid and his wife, I guess, so I went to a group home."

"Then what?" He kept his tone gentle as they stood side-by-side in the aisle.

"Other foster homes, or group homes." She glanced away, but he didn't think she was seeing the plants in the greenhouse. "I stopped trying to keep track of how many. I changed schools constantly. Made friends just to leave again. Until I stopped trying."

"For friends?" What she described sounded like a lonely way to grow up. He'd been surrounded by family. His sisters and their friends had filled the house with life and noise.

"Not only friends, but any connections. I never had connections to people or communities. I got used to being on my own." She stopped, her face stony as her fingers curled around the edge of the cart. "Thomas never wanted me to have friends, either. He didn't even want me to leave the house unless I was with him. I should have realized sooner that he was intentionally isolating me, but I was so accustomed to being alone that it didn't register as a warning sign. I was hoping, after Sebastian contacted me…"

He put his hand over hers, keeping his touch light: comforting, not controlling. He could guess what she'd been hoping for. If Sebastian had lived, they would have rebuilt a sibling bond, and she wouldn't have been adrift anymore.

She gave her head a little shake. "How'd we get here?"

"Next to the pansies?" he asked with a gentle smile. She returned it and bumped her shoulder against his, a silent thank-you for changing the subject.

"Is that what these are?" She touched the petals. "They have sweet faces."

"You could put some of those in pots on the front porch," he suggested. "They don't mind the cooler temperatures we still have at night."

"Then I think I'll get some." She selected purple-and-yellow pansies and put them in the cart. "What else will work?"

"How about some calendulas?" He pointed ahead of them to bright orange and yellow flowers.

"They look like daisies, but with more petals," she said, moving toward them. "I *can* identify a daisy."

"I never said you couldn't." He helped her select several plants that looked healthy and vibrant.

"I want to grow tomatoes and cucumbers, too," she commented when they were done in the flowers.

"Those are a little further on." He gestured ahead to a connected greenhouse. "But it's too early for most vegetables to be in the ground, and you don't have a good place for a vegetable patch. Too much shade in the backyard."

"See, I didn't even know that. I've got a lot to learn. There must be enough sunny ground for just a few plants, though." She had a capacity for hope that kept surprising him. The tea party yesterday and her attitude now.

"Maybe, but you might want to keep in mind that vegetables take a lot of tending. By later in the summer, will you want to be working in the garden?"

"You might be right about that." She glanced down. Her pregnancy wasn't visible yet, but it would be soon. "We can look at the plants, though, right? I just want to see, and I won't have you around forever to give me pointers."

"Two more weeks," he said.

She blinked as if the time frame surprised her. It shouldn't, since he'd told her from the beginning when he was leaving. "I'd forgotten it was so soon."

Her words made him wonder if she'd miss him when he left. He would miss her, he realized. Before he returned to base, he wanted another chance to kiss her. Their kiss over the child-sized table had swept through him, knocking him off-balance. He wasn't interested in a serious relationship, and he assumed she wasn't, either, but what if they could have… *something*?

7

———————

arley was sitting on the top step of the porch, enjoying the late morning air. She'd get porch furniture eventually—a swing and maybe a wicker settee and chair—but for now the step did nicely. It was becoming her happy place. When she took breaks from work, she tended to wander out there and sit down.

It had been a good day so far. Garrett had gone with her to see the attorney. She'd begun the divorce paperwork, and Mr. Burke had suggested pursuing a restraining order for additional protection if Thomas found out where she was. Harley had agreed. It felt good to be taking action, taking her life back. She wanted to leave Thomas in her past as she built her future here. She glanced over her shoulder at the house, which was slowly becoming just the home she'd always wanted. Thanks in no small part to Garrett. She'd miss him when he left: miss his companionship every bit as much as his drive to work on the house.

His kiss, though. She couldn't stop thinking about it.

She cautioned herself about getting attached to him. He was kind and caring and felt safe, but he'd be gone soon. She needed to find her way back to being independent. Thomas had taken that from her, so it was up to her to regain it. She could start small. A trip to a coffee shop in downtown Hartsville might be just the thing.

She went inside, got her purse, and let Garrett know she was going. He was using a shop vac to clean up the construction area in the kitchen where he'd reframed the entrance to the secret room that would become a large pantry, but he paused to give her a thumbs-up and smile at her.

Downtown, she found a parking space and entered the coffee shop.

"Hi, welcome to the Hart of Coffee Café," a young woman behind the counter said.

"Thanks." Harley looked at the menu and the display case full of pastries before placing her order.

"I haven't seen you in before," the barista commented as she worked on Harley's order.

"I just moved to town," Harley said. She didn't want to go into the particulars of inheriting her brother's home, so she kept it simple.

"Welcome again." The woman smiled. "We're a friendly place."

"That's been my experience so far." Everyone she'd met had been pleasant.

"You might want to follow the town's social media pages. Oh, and the library's, too. They have some good programs."

"Good idea. I need to meet people." Harley wasn't sure what prompted her to say that to a stranger. It just came out.

"There's a bulletin board over there." The barista gestured to the back wall. "It has all sorts of information on community events and such."

After getting her double chocolate decaf mocha with extra foam, Harley went to look at the board. There were notices about cats and dogs who needed homes. That might not be a bad idea in the future. She'd never had a pet. Other flyers advertised items for sale, and some indicated groups that were open to new members. A bookstore sponsored a monthly book club meeting, and a yarn store welcomed people who wanted to learn to knit or crochet on Thursday evenings.

She could see herself doing that. Maybe she could make something for the baby and meet some people.

"Thanks," she said to the barista on her way out.

"Wait. We like to give new customers a little gift." The woman handed her a mug with the café's logo printed on it. "You can bring it with you when you come next time, and we'll give you a discount on your drink."

After thanking the woman again, Harley walked out onto the street and took a minute to study the other shops nearby. She would need to buy a few items of clothing soon and was pleased to spot a boutique that looked nice. Another day, she'd come back.

Harley drove home feeling good about where she was in life. She'd wanted a relationship with her brother, and she wouldn't get that… but even in death, he'd changed everything for her by giving her the house and the means to leave Thomas. She was determined not to waste the opportunity.

She had struggles ahead of her. No doubt about that. But she felt stronger, more capable, than she had in a long time. She'd take it one thing at a time, she decided as she drove back to her house. Even thinking those words—her house—was starting to feel more normal.

She pulled up short, though, when she saw three cars she didn't recognize parked in the driveway. Her first fear was that Thomas had found her. Since he worked as a used car salesman, he tended to change cars frequently. Her nerves calmed when she saw the vehicles all had South Carolina license plates.

Then she spotted three women on the porch with Garrett and recognized one of them as Imogen, who, along with her husband, had brought groceries last week. The other two were strangers. As Harley got out of her car, she caught Garrett's reassuring smile and nod. Since she trusted him, she walked forward, even though the situation made her jittery.

"Hello," she called.

"Sorry to just show up, but we wanted to bring you a welcome basket," Imogen replied and then introduced Mia and Violet, who Harley learned were also the wives of SEALs from Hartsville. Apparently, their husbands had been friends since they were kids, and they still served together as SEALs. They'd all known her brother, even though he'd been on a different team.

"Come in," Harley said. She led them into the living room that Garrett had completed a few days earlier. He and Patrick had hauled a sofa, chair, and coffee table out of storage, so the room was furnished enough for her guests to sit. "I didn't expect anything, but thanks."

"Go ahead and open it," Mia said after putting the basket on the table.

Harley peeled away the cellophane to reveal a variety of gifts: kitchen items like towels and cooking utensils, a scented candle, a small print of a mountain vista she recognized as being nearby, mason jars with the ingredients for cookies already measured, and a few books. One was a baby book with soft corners and a rattle attached, and another was a book about pregnancy.

"Garrett told us—or, rather, he told Patrick—about the baby," Imogen explained. "I hope you don't mind."

"No, it's fine." She hadn't said it was a secret, and it was probably good that others knew she was expecting. She did wonder what else Garrett had revealed about her, though. "This is really kind of you."

"You're part of the SEAL family now. We take care of our own," Mia said.

Harley was about to object, since she and Garrett weren't in a relationship, but then she realized Mia was referring to Sebastian.

"Garrett's been busy," Violet commented. "I was here just two weeks ago, and this room was a wreck. I can't believe how he's pulled it together."

"He doesn't slow down," Harley agreed. "He's trying to get so many things done before he leaves."

"He told us that would be soon," Imogen said. "We want you to know that you won't be alone. You'll have us, and we all have experience with babies, so we'll be happy to help out."

Harley tried to thank them again, but they began chatting about pregnancy and its weird symptoms before she could. It was nice to talk with other women, and by the time they left, she felt more comfortable around them. She even accepted an invitation to a cookout and gave them her phone number. Violet immediately started a group text. The women's confident, assertive approach to friendship was a bit startling, but she was willing to give it a try. It had been a good day so far, one that gave her hope that her future would be different from her past.

After she waved goodbye to them from the porch, she walked into the kitchen to find Garrett. He had a paintbrush in his hand and was putting a coat of a sunny yellow color on the wall he'd just redone. The color made her do a double take. It was beautiful. So happy and bright.

"Sebastian bought the paint before… before our last mission. I prob-ably should have asked before I started. I hope the color is all right with you." He paused with the paintbrush suspended over the bucket.

"I love it." With the fresh paint and the light oak cabinets, the kitchen glowed. But… wait a minute. She returned to the living room and grabbed the towels and oven mitts from the gift basket. They were covered in yellow flowers the exact color of the wall. Someone had given her visitors inside information. She walked back to the kitchen with the items in her hand.

"Something wrong?" Garrett asked.

"You called them, didn't you? That's how they knew what to get."

"When Imogen called *me*," he said, "I told her that the kitchen was going to be yellow. That was yesterday evening. I had no idea the three of them would move so quickly. Is it okay with you?"

He sounded nervous, and she forced herself to take a deep breath and relax. Thomas was always so secretive, having conversations she wasn't allowed to overhear. It had made her sensitive about the idea of people talking behind her back. But Garrett's explanation made sense—and, really, what had been the harm in telling the women the kitchen would be yellow? She loved the dish towels and oven mitts they'd picked out. "Yes, it's nice."

"Good. I want you to be at home here."

"I'm starting to feel that way." She didn't add *thanks to you*, but it was how she felt. She kept her gaze on him. The truth of her words simultaneously scared her and made her happy. Happiness was winning out over the fear and uncertainty she'd gotten used to, and it was partly due to Garrett. She wanted him to know that, but it was hard for her to say it. She'd been burned too many times.

"Objective achieved, then," he said after a pause long enough for her to wonder what he was thinking. He had to be aware of the attraction between them. The kiss in the playroom proved that. But would he act on those feelings again? Paint dripped from his brush into the bucket, which seemed to bring him back to the moment. "I think I'm going to accomplish my other objectives, too. Projects are getting ticked off my list pretty quickly."

"Because you're working so hard. I wish you'd let me help more." She'd tried to, but he was cautious about letting her take on too much. Strangely, she didn't take it as him putting limits on her. He was looking out for her.

"You've got other things to worry about."

He was right about that. He was right about a lot of things. She'd misjudged men in the past, but she was sure he was a good one. She took a step closer to Garrett. A spark traveled between them, and she knew she was going to kiss him.

He put his paintbrush down and moved toward her. They met, and she had the fleeting idea that maybe this time, if she took a chance, things would work out. With him. She was still processing that thought when Garrett's arms went around her waist and he drew her closer.

This kiss was different from their first. That one had started slow. This one exploded as soon as their lips met. She looped her arms around Garrett's neck and enjoyed the contact between their bodies as he explored her mouth like he couldn't get enough of her. She had no sense of time passing until he broke from her lips to kiss along her jaw and down her neck. It was heaven to be held safe in his arms while passion rose between them.

Her fingers moved to his shoulders, where she felt his muscles through the thin fabric of his T-shirt. She wanted to rip it away and explore him for real, feel his warm skin. He shifted them, stepping back but taking her with him. He sat in a kitchen chair and pulled her down to straddle him. Everything felt incredible… until the chair scooted a few inches and Garrett broke the kiss with a curse.

"What?" Her tone was dreamy. She felt dreamy.

"The paint." He nodded to the side. The movement of the chair had bumped the paint tray, slopping paint onto an old rug. "I'd better get that before it seeps through onto the floor."

He lifted her off his lap, which was the only place she wanted to be, and set her down in another chair. Before he turned to clean up the paint, though, he held her face between his hands, his thumbs stroking over her cheeks. "I want to continue this later… but only if you want it, too."

Her heart thudded in her chest, because that was the perfect thing for him to say. She'd been powerless too often in her life. Garrett seemed to understand and respect that.

"I do."

He smiled then, a charming grin, and she fell for him a little more.

8

"Keep us company in the kitchen," Imogen said, taking Harley's arm, when Harley and Garrett arrived at the cook-out. "Garrett, the guys are in the backyard, grilling the meat."

"And drinking beer," Violet added.

"Not too much beer, I hope, since they're in charge of the kids," Mia added. "Go on, Garrett. Matthew's out there, too. He'll be glad to see you." She took the bowl of fruit salad Garrett had brought and shooed him away.

Garrett gave Harley a look, a silent, "Is this okay?"

She gave him a smile, even though she wasn't a hundred percent comfortable. These women were kind, but she had counted on Garrett sticking closer to her side.

"We'll take good care of her," Imogen assured him. "I promise."

Harley peeked into the living room as they walked down the hall. The house wasn't large, but it was clearly well loved and appeared to be happily lived-in. Harley particularly liked the white lace curtains and colorful, mismatched throw pillows on the sofa.

"I love to sew," Imogen explained. "Patrick thinks we have too many pillows, but I enjoy making them. Some of the fabric is vintage, from when his grandmother lived here."

"The house has been in his family all that time?" Having a home passed down through generations was so different from Harley's life experience.

"For nearly a hundred years. We're thinking about adding on soon."

"You are?" Mia asked, narrowing her eyes. "Is there a reason?"

Imogen smiled. "We're going to need another bedroom and probably another bathroom, with the baby coming." Her announcement was met with squeals from Mia and Violet. Mia pulled them all in for a group hug.

"Two more babies to spoil," Mia said. "How delightful."

"Only two?" Imogen shot Mia and Violet a look.

"We're trying," Violet said. "I got pregnant with Nate even though we very much *not* trying, but things aren't moving as fast this time around."

"It'll happen. Just give it time." Mia looped an arm around Violet's waist.

"What about you?" Violet asked. "You and Kenton have been married for, what, four months? Is it too soon?"

"Not for me, but you know Kenton." Mia rolled her eyes, but she was smiling. "He has spreadsheets detailing when everything should happen." She laughed. "But I'm working on him to move up his timetable. I told him I'd already disrupted his life plan so much that he might as well toss it out the window."

"You're good for him," Imogen said as they reached the kitchen. "He needs a little chaos in his life."

"He got that with me and the girls. I'm raising my twin nieces," Mia explained to Harley. "My sister and brother-in-law died in a car accident, and Emma and Ava became mine."

"I'm very sorry about your family, but your nieces are lucky to have you," Harley said. How different her own life would have been if she'd had an aunt or grandparent who could take her in.

"I'm lucky to have them," Mia said. "I love them to pieces. Okay, what needs to get finished before we join the guys?"

"I need to finish cutting up the vegetables for the salad," Imogen said. "Do you want to arrange the cookies you brought on a serving tray?"

"On it."

"Violet, can you pour the chips in those bowls and get the dip from the fridge?"

"Happy to."

"What about me?" Harley asked. "How can I help?"

"Just sit down and tell us how the home renovations are going. Patrick said something about discovering a room you didn't know was there. How'd that happen?"

Harley sat in the chair Imogen pointed to and told the story about the playroom and the items they found in there. She skipped over the kiss. These were smart women and probably guessed that there was something between her and Garrett, but she wasn't comfortable sharing personal information. It was easier to talk about the tea set and her plans for the pantry. They asked questions, encouraging her to continue when she would otherwise have concluded quickly.

It amazed her how comfortable and included she felt with these women. They were close to her age and happy to live in Hartsville. The longer she was here, the more she thought she could be happy here, too. It was a friendly place and seemed like the kind of community that valued relationships and families.

The conversation soon turned to the other women's kids. They had five between them. She focused on remembering names and ages.

"Uh-oh, Ava and Emma are using Garrett like a jungle gym," Mia said, looking out the window toward the yard. "We should go rescue the poor man. My girls can be relentless, and they adore him."

Harley went to the window and smiled. Two adorable girls were climbing all over Garrett while he laughed and playfully ruffled their hair. The sight made something melt inside her.

Garrett saw faces in the kitchen window, but he only got a quick peek before Emma tackled him again. He was happy to get down on the ground with the girls. He liked playing with the kids and hanging with his buddies while the burgers grilled. He even liked Patrick and Imogen's giant dog, Mr. Bubblesworth, who was running circles around them, wagging his tail. At times like this, he wished he lived closer to his own family. Whenever he got back to Idaho, he had a blast with his nieces and nephews.

"Girls," Kenton called, "let Garrett up."

"Let's play house," Ellery suggested, and the younger kids ran to follow her into the small structure that Patrick had built for his daughter.

Garrett got to his feet and went to sit next to Matthew at the picnic table.

"Those girls have a ton of energy," his teammate said. Matthew was staying with Mia and Kenton while he healed from his latest surgery and waited to see what would be in store for physical therapy and rehabilitation.

"That they do," Garrett agreed. "Have they been running you ragged? You look tired." His voice dropped lower, to give them a bit more privacy for the conversation. "Is it your hand? Have there been any new problems?"

Matthew shrugged. "Nothing new—just the same pain and stiffness. But it'll heal." Neither Garrett nor Matthew was sure of that, considering the extent of the burns and broken bones he'd suffered. "I'm not giving up. I'm going to deal with this and be back on the team. But, Jesus, it's hard waiting around. I like it here in Hartsville, but it's not where I want to be."

"I get that." Garrett felt the same way. He'd gotten comfortable in the small town, but it wasn't home to him, either.

Soon enough, he'd be headed back to base, which brought on a different set of worries. He didn't like the idea of leaving Harley on her own. He told himself that he was simply concerned about Thomas finding and harming her because Sebastian would want him to make sure she was safe.

After the kisses he and Harley had shared over the past few days, though, that might not be the whole truth. They'd kept it to just kisses, so far, even if he'd been tempted to do more. He wanted her, but he was leaving soon and she was emotionally fragile, which wasn't a good combination.

"Hey, guys, I need a favor," he said.

"Anything," Anderson responded, speaking for the group.

"I'm worried about Harley's safety after I leave Hartsville."

"Has she gotten more threats from her loser ex?" Patrick asked. Garrett had filled them all in about the calls and messages Harley kept receiving and how she was pursuing a divorce and a restraining order.

"They keep coming," he said. "I put in a doorbell camera last week, but it's not enough. She needs a sophisticated security system, and that's not my area of expertise."

"I've got some experience with those and know a few guys I can call on if needed," Patrick volunteered.

"I can give you a hand with installation," Matthew said, lifting his uninjured one. "Singular, not plural." Matthew's humor was dark, but they all chuckled.

"I'd appreciate that." Garrett knew they'd come through for him.

"We can all look out for her while you're on base, too," Anderson offered. "Her husband still doesn't know where she's at, right?"

"So far, and I hope it stays that way, but I don't trust the situation. If he comes after her..." Garrett didn't need to finish the sentence, because they all knew it would be ugly.

"She's Sebastian's sister, man. We've got her back," Kenton said. "And yours, too, if you need it."

The door from the kitchen opened just then, and Harley followed the other women out. Garrett saw the reluctance on her face. She'd gotten comfortable with him, but she still distrusted strangers, particularly men. Of the group gathered, she'd only met Patrick so far.

Garrett went to her side. He was tempted to take her hand, but they weren't exactly a couple, so he settled for a light touch on her arm before introducing her to Matthew, Anderson, and Kenton. All three of them turned on the charm and had Harley smiling quickly.

"Okay, guys, round up the kids, and let's eat," Imogen called. There was a flurry of activity for a few minutes, but soon everyone was seated at a table, heaping plates in front of them.

"How's it going?" Garrett whispered as he sat next to Harley and handed her a bottle of water.

"Fine. Everyone is so nice."

He hated that she sounded so surprised about that. The world hadn't been kind to her, but he saw that changing here in Hartsville. He might not be around to see it, though.

The thought of leaving Hartsville gave him a pang. He was reluctant to go because of Harley, but he'd gotten attached to the sense of community here, too. He'd had that growing up and hadn't realized how much he missed it.

"You'll have a lot of friends in Hartsville," he said.

"Guess so." She glanced around at the other couples. "It doesn't seem quite real to me."

Anderson and Violet's son made a break for it just then and dashed across the yard with his dad chasing after him. Anderson scooped up the boy and tickled his belly until he shrieked with laughter.

"It's real," Garrett said, turning back to Harley. "You've landed in a good place."

He didn't let himself think about how it would feel to leave this place —and her—behind.

9

Garrett took her hand as they walked home from the party that evening. The early spring air had a chill to it, but her fingers felt warm in his. She squeezed, letting him know that she was glad to be with him.

"Did you have fun?" he asked. "It looked like you were enjoying yourself."

"I did." After eating, they'd lingered at the table and talked. She'd held Patrick and Imogen's son while he'd fallen asleep, which had been the sweetest moment of the day for her. She couldn't wait to hold her own child. She'd been excited about the baby before, but seeing the families made her long for that life even more.

She'd have it, or at least part of it. She and her child would be a family. She stole a look at Garrett from under her lashes. What if she could have more with him? She shouldn't be thinking that way, but after a glimpse of a different life, it was tempting to dream. And why not dream big?

"I don't think I've ever been to a party like that before," she mused. "Thomas would sometimes take me to the club where he was a part-time bouncer, but that was only ever about showing off and one-upping the other guys." She'd hated those nights. "He wanted me to dress a certain way, do my hair and makeup, so I looked the part of the perfect wife."

"He didn't let you talk to anyone, though, did he?" Garrett was almost too perceptive.

"Not really." She'd made that mistake one night and gotten into a conversation with a group of friends celebrating a birthday—a mix of men and women. Just when she was starting to feel comfortable with them, Thomas had swooped in and declared they were going home. She shuddered when she recalled what happened as soon as they were in the car.

Garrett must have sensed her reaction. He stopped walking and pulled her into a gentle hug, running his hand down her back to soothe her. She rested her head against his shoulder, feeling safe in his arms rather than trapped.

"He hurt you," Garrett murmured. "I hope you know I never will." He kissed her hair, but she could only nod. She couldn't voice the words she was feeling—her regret for having not seen what Thomas was to begin with and then not leaving him once she knew. It was too late for regrets now. All she could do was move forward and make better choices. Like being with Garrett.

She was grateful for the opportunity to make her own decisions now. That made her feel younger, more hopeful. She tilted her face up to Garrett's. "Thank you for taking me to the cookout today."

He chuckled. "Like I could have shown up without you. They like you, Harley. So do I." He kissed her then, but he ended it far too soon.

"Is that all I get?" she teased. It had been ages since she'd said anything even mildly flirtatious. It felt good.

"Until we get home. Then, it's whatever you want."

There it was again. She had the choice, and it was an easy one. "I want you." Even in the dim light, she saw his immediate smile.

"Glad to hear that." He put his arm around her waist, getting them moving again. When they reached the house, they ran up the porch steps, and he quickly worked the lock. As soon as they were inside, they came together.

She'd enjoyed their other kisses, but now she realized that she'd been holding back, protecting a part of herself out of fear. She let that go and gave herself over to the kiss—to Garrett.

After what could have been forever or only a few seconds, he broke the kiss and rested his forehead against hers. "Harley, I have to know you're sure about this before we go upstairs."

"I'm sure. Make love with me, Garrett." He looked at her a long second, and his eyes held emotions she didn't even know how to name. Before she drew another breath, she was cradled in his arms as he headed for the stairs.

In her bedroom, he gently put her on her feet and worked her sweatshirt over her head. She reached for the hem of her tank top, wanting to get rid of any barrier between them, but he caught her hands in his.

"Please, let me undress you. I want to memorize every second of this." His palms slid under her shirt and coasted up her back, slowly taking the top with them. When it was off, he paused to look at her. "You're so beautiful, Harley. I thought so the minute I first saw you."

"You did?" She remembered those moments in the lawyer's office. She'd been too nervous and upset to notice much about Garrett except his intimidating size.

"Yeah." His fingers stroked lightly over her breasts through her bra until her nipples grew hard. "I just didn't expect…" He didn't need to finish the sentence. Neither of them had expected their growing connection.

She took his face in her hands and kissed him, letting him know that words were no longer necessary. They continued undressing each other slowly as their kisses deepened. Once they were in bed, they lay on their sides, their bodies pressed tightly together. His hand brushed the curve of her breast and coasted down her side.

He moaned when she slipped her hand between them and stroked his erection. "So good," he murmured. Her fingers tightened around him. "Can't. Not yet." He caught her hand and brought it to his lips, kissing it before rolling her onto her back. He covered her body with his, hovering just above her and holding her gaze. "I want this to be perfect for you."

"It already is." She arched up and kissed him again, loving the feel of his erection against her stomach, the warmth where his skin brushed hers. She wanted him more than she'd ever wanted anyone, but the slow pace suited her.

She made a sound of protest when he broke their kiss—she wanted that contact with him. But then he took her nipple into his mouth and sucked on it, and any ability to speak disappeared. He did the same to the other breast before trailing kisses down her body to the tops of her thighs and back up. When his lips reconnected with hers, his hands parted her legs and cupped the moist heat there.

He stroked her sensitive nub as his tongue tangled with hers, overwhelming her with sensation. She spread her legs wider, inviting him in, and he slid a finger into her. Combined with the other stimulation, it was exactly what she needed, and she was tipping over into shivers of bliss before she knew it. He kept kissing her—long, soothing kisses —but they were far from done.

"I want you inside me." Pleasure still pulsing through her, she lifted her hips to rub herself against his erection.

"Be right back, sweetheart." He kissed her forehead and got out of bed. She pushed up on her elbows to watch him walk away to his bedroom across the hall. That was a sight she'd never forget. Tight butt and long, lean muscles defining his legs and back. When he returned, she decided that the front was even better. A few visible scars reminded her that he was a warrior, but with her, he'd been nothing but gentle and loving.

He tore open the condom and quickly rolled it on before rejoining her on the bed. She wrapped her legs around his hips, letting him know she was ready for him. He pushed into her, slowly at first, until he was fully in.

"Okay?" he whispered. She clamped her inner muscles around his shaft in answer.

After that, words no longer mattered as they moved together, the passion building even higher between them. She was close to coming again when he reached between them and caressed her clit. That was all it took to have her crying out. Seconds later, his powerful body shuddered with his release as he said her name over and over.

Being with him was the best feeling she'd ever known—not just the sex, but all the rest of it, too. When he left the bed to dispose of the condom, she missed him. He was back soon and slid into bed beside her, spooning his body around hers and kissing her neck and shoulder. She dozed off, safe and content. She didn't know how long she slept before Garrett's voice woke her.

"Are you hungry?" he asked. His hand was flat on her stomach. "I can feel rumbling in there." Just then, her stomach growled. "Or is that the baby?"

"I'm hungry," she said. It was too early to feel the baby's movements. "I ate plenty at the party, but I seem to be burning through food. That's new this week." The pregnancy was bringing constant changes to her body.

"Any requests? I'll make you a snack and bring it up." He kissed her shoulder again before rising and grabbing for his jeans.

She instantly missed the warm contact, but she *was* hungry. "I'll come with you. You don't need to wait on me."

"But I want to," he said, and their gazes met. He was so very different from the people in her past.

She appreciated that, but she got out of bed and pulled on his discarded T-shirt. It fell nearly to her knees, a reminder of his size. That had scared her at first, but she knew now that she had nothing to fear from him. He could be dangerous—there was no question about that—but not to her. In every one of their interactions, he was protective and caring.

"Looks good on you." He was grinning. "Come here."

She went willingly. Their kiss lasted until he started to lift the edge of the shirt. She playfully swatted his hands away. "Hungry, remember."

"I'm not denying a pregnant woman food." He took her hand as they left the room. "What sounds good?"

"Peanut butter, which is weird since I'm not a huge fan of it." But she'd found that her tastes had changed.

In the kitchen, they cut up apples and celery to dip in the peanut butter. While they ate, she opened the home decorating magazine dedicated to nurseries that he'd brought her. She'd marked a few pages and flipped back to those to take another look. Imogen and Violet had given her numerous suggestions about setting up the nursery, and she was anxious to do some planning.

"I like this." She turned the magazine to show Garrett a built-in unit that included a diaper-changing area and several small drawers, perfect for storing baby clothes.

He studied the image for a minute. "You still plan to use the small room off your bedroom?"

"I think it's the perfect space for a nursery." It could be a lovely space, and the convenience couldn't be beat.

"I could build that for you," he said, "and I'd make it so it could be converted to more traditional closet storage when the baby outgrows the nursery."

"That's a good idea. I'd love that, but you don't have time before you go." His departure date was looming closer and closer, a fact that she didn't wish to dwell on.

"I've got to report in just over a week," he said, "but I'm not being deployed overseas."

"You're not?" she asked, feeling instantly hopeful. He hadn't mentioned anything about that.

"I got an email this morning with my new assignment. They've got me training recruits." His brow wrinkled when he said the words.

"You don't want to do that?"

"Training is fine, but this isn't about my skill in running drills. I'm being kept on American soil because the investigation into my last mission is ongoing. They just won't say that's the reason."

"Oh, I'm sorry…"

"It's fine," he said quickly. "The good part is that I'll only be five hours from here. I could come down on weekends and continue the house projects."

"And be with me?" She was far more interested in that than the work he might do.

He hesitated a moment before saying, "Yeah, I'd like that." He fell silent again. Something was going on inside him.

"Would you?" she prompted, surprising herself. The old Harley wouldn't have pushed him. She'd have been scared to. "You're not sounding very convincing."

He covered her hand where it lay on the table, but it still took him a minute to start talking. "My last mission…" He paused and looked away. "I'm sorry, Harley, but I… It's my fault Sebastian died."

"That can't be." She didn't believe him for a second. While she waited for him to tell the story, she turned her hand over and gripped his in silent encouragement.

"He was like a brother to me. We trained together, served together. He was the best man I've ever known, and I'm proud to have been his teammate and friend. There's no one I trusted more, and I think he felt the same about me." He swallowed. "And that's what got him killed."

"Tell me what happened." She'd known Garrett was on that mission, but she hadn't asked for details. She hadn't been ready to hear the story. Truthfully, she wasn't sure she was ready yet, but Garrett seemed like he needed to talk about it.

"Well, I can't tell you much about the specifics," he began. "But… Sebastian and I had been up for more than twenty-four hours doing recon for a planned raid. When we got back to our team and reported in, they'd gotten new intel that moved up the time frame. I wanted to be involved when we moved in, even though he and I were both tired. No way would he let me go without him, so he volunteered to be part of the action, too." Harley put her other hand on top of Garrett's, giving him what reassurance she could. "If he hadn't been there…

he'd still be alive. He'd be here for you, and… and I wouldn't have lost the person I was closest to in the world."

When she saw the glimmer of tears in his eyes, she got up and went to him. She put her arms around him and let him bury his face against her shoulder, just as he'd done for her earlier when she'd sought comfort.

Harley had thought there was nothing she could do for Garrett, but she could see she'd been wrong. His grief was strong, maybe stronger than hers. She hadn't known Sebastian very well at all, so her sadness over the loss of him was more for what couldn't be. Garrett's was for what had been.

"Garrett," she said, lifting his chin so she could look into his eyes, "you've got to listen to me. You can't blame yourself for Sebastian's death. You couldn't have known what was going to happen that day. Sebastian was an adult, a trained SEAL. He made his choice, the same as you did."

"But he wouldn't have—"

She put her fingers over his lips. "Don't torment yourself. Would Sebastian want you do to that? I didn't know him well, but I don't think he would." The man she'd met through emails and that one Zoom didn't seem the type to hold a grudge against the people he loved.

"He wouldn't," Garrett admitted, but she could see that he was still struggling, so she gave him a soft kiss.

"Should we go back to bed?" She was tired, but she wanted him near her, wanted to hold him.

"You go ahead," he said. "I'll clean up here and join you soon."

She nodded, knowing that he needed time to himself. Just then, her phone buzzed with a message.

She checked the screen and gasped. The text was from Thomas—and it was an image of Sebastian's house. Her home. "Oh God, he's found me." More messages poured in, reminding her of the power Thomas had over her.

"How?" Garrett was on his feet beside her, staring down at the screen.

"I don't know. I was so careful—or I thought I was." She swallowed, trying to keep the panic at bay.

"But he's not here. That picture of the house is from Google Maps."

"Right." She took a breath. "He works two jobs, so his schedule is really rigid. He can't just take off without notice." She was reassuring herself, but she hoped she wasn't being delusional. Would Thomas risk his jobs to come after her? His work was important to him, but he could be unpredictable. No one knew that better than she did. His mood could swing from loving to violent in seconds. "But he will come." The messages made that clear. "He's still technically my husband." Every doubt she'd ever had about escaping from Thomas returned.

"You've started the divorce. You are legally separated. He has no power over you." Garrett's voice was calm, but it didn't temper her fear. "And I made plans this evening with Patrick and Matthew to put in a sophisticated security system here. It'll help keep you safe."

She knew he'd protect her if he could, but he wouldn't always be around. He had to return to his base, and even if he came back on weekends, there would be long stretches without him. She wanted to trust in the safety Garrett offered, but Thomas had shattered any sense of safety she'd managed to find before. And she very much feared he was about to do so again.

10

"I like this better than what we saw at the last place," Matthew commented, pointing to one of the security systems on the shelf of the big-box store. "I did some research and looked over the materials Patrick sent. This one offers better video quality and can be adjusted to be more sensitive to movement."

Patrick had told him the best way to get a system in place quickly was to buy components and build one, versus contracting with a company that might not be able to install it right away. Patrick had promised to help out and call on his connections to make sure the system operated seamlessly.

"We'll want that," Garrett agreed. "I don't want anyone sneaking up on the house. I'm worried about the trees in the yard, though. Will they throw off the sensors if it's windy?"

"Yeah, they could, from what I've read," Matthew said. "That's why Patrick recommends one like this that picks up body heat as well. It's more expensive, but it's worth it."

"I don't give a crap what it costs." Garrett glanced at Harley, who was farther down the aisle. She'd stopped to look at baby monitors, which gave him an idea. "Is there a way to integrate baby monitors into the system?"

"Probably. It might be tricky to control it all from the same app, but I suppose it's possible." Matthew balanced a box from the system they were looking at on his good hand so he could read the specs more carefully. He seemed to be adapting to his injury, but Garrett knew that he wasn't happy about it—nor the fact that his career was hanging in the balance.

"Have they decided on a physical therapy regimen yet?" Garrett asked.

"Not yet," Matthew answered. "They say it's too soon, need to heal more first, yadda yadda. It's frustrating, all the waiting. You know I'll do whatever it takes—if they'd just let me get started." He was always the positive force on their team. The first one to crack a joke and break the tension, or yell, "Hell, yeah, we can do that."

"If you need anything, you let me know." Garrett could only hope that Matthew would call on him. He wanted his buddy back in fighting condition.

"Looks to me like you've got your hands full at the moment." Matthew grinned at him.

Garrett couldn't help looking toward Harley again. She was putting one box back on the shelf and grabbing a second. He had to fight the urge to rush over and help her.

"Got to admit I never saw this coming," Matthew said.

"What?" Garrett swung his head back to his friend.

"You getting serious about a woman. You'll be turning into a family man soon, even though you've always said you didn't want that. You were married to the job, remember? Hell, there's been a couple times I thought we'd have to have a ceremony with flowers and a cake, you've been so damn committed to the Navy."

"I'm still committed to being a SEAL," Garrett said. That hadn't changed. "But, yeah, I never saw this coming, either."

"So how are you going to handle leaving?" Matthew asked. "You've got your assignment, right?"

"Stateside training on base," Garrett confirmed. "I can travel back and forth on weekends to be with Harley."

"That'll work for now, but what about when you're on a new assignment that has you halfway around the globe and cut off for weeks at a time?"

That was a problem Garrett didn't have a solution for. He'd thought about it, but he'd stopped himself from going too far down that path. For one thing, he didn't know what Harley wanted. They'd talked far into the night and made love again. But, even though she'd implied that she wanted him around, she was cautious, too. He couldn't blame her for that. She'd been burned and was still dealing with the aftermath of a devastating relationship.

"Not sure yet," he said. "I guess the only thing I know is that I'll go. Being a SEAL is what I am."

"Same." Matthew lost his characteristic good humor for a moment. "I just wish I could speed up the recovery process somehow..."

"Don't say you'd work harder, because you probably couldn't."

Matthew cracked a smile. "True enough. I'm pushing it as much as the doctors will let me. I'm getting back out there, come hell or high water."

"Damn straight," Garrett said.

"Speaking of which, I've got to split—I have a call scheduled with one of the base doctors. I'm trying to get them to okay some kind of exercise, at least. I think they're getting sick of me, to be honest. But go ahead and get this system—it looks good to me. I'll be over ASAP to help with the install." Matthew headed for the exit, stopping briefly to say goodbye to Harley, who smiled at him. Matthew was a likable guy, even when he was hurting. Garrett was glad there were people who'd be sticking around the area for now that she could rely on. Any of the SEALs would look out for her. He didn't doubt that.

He needed, though, to have a conversation with Harley about where they were going. Were they a couple in any real sense? Was she willing to be a military girlfriend—or even wife? That was a tough role to take on. What he had with Harley didn't feel casual, though. For him, it was very intense and very real. She'd taken some hard knocks in life, and he wanted to be the one who gave her the happiness she deserved.

She came toward him, looking pleased, less like the world was sitting on her shoulders. And, damn, she was beautiful.

"Ready to purchase?" she asked.

"I texted Patrick some questions, and I'm waiting to hear back from him. If he gives his approval, I'll come back and pick up what we need." He put his arm around her waist as they headed for the exit. "Is there anything else you want while we're out?"

"Ice cream," she declared. "I want a chocolate milkshake so much that I don't think I can live another moment without one. Ridiculous cravings. Do you know a good ice cream place in the area?"

"Dairy Dock." He'd been there before with Patrick and his kids. "It's the best around."

They went out to his truck, and he drove back into the center of Hartsville, where the ice cream shop was located.

"Thanks," she said out of the blue when he'd pulled into a parking space. "You're so good to me."

He hated that she sounded surprised. "You don't need to thank me, Harley. I'm here to support you with whatever you need."

"I'm sure my brother didn't mean for you to be dealing with a pregnancy when he asked you to look out for me." Some of her nervousness was back.

"I would have done everything I could to fulfill Sebastian's request in any case, but"—he took her hand—"I'm with you because I want to be." He didn't know how to express more than that, but her face brightened and she leaned closer to kiss him. The kiss was brief, but it seemed to confirm that she was happy with what they had going.

"Now, ice cream." She pulled away. "I'm starving."

"You go sit in the sun while I stand in line," he suggested.

The warmth of the day had brought out plenty of people eager for a treat. Families sat at the picnic tables in front of the ice cream stand. Harley found one close to the street that was unoccupied. For a moment, she closed her eyes, enjoying the feel of the sunshine on her face.

And she was marveling just a bit, too. How, in less than two weeks, had she gone from being afraid to allow Garrett to stay in her house to not wanting him to leave? She'd trusted too readily before, but now that she was in a relationship with a good man, she realized that she should have seen the signs with Thomas. His charm had never been more than a veneer that had turned her head. With Garrett there was no pretense. He was exactly what he seemed. He couldn't be faking it, not with the circle of friends that he had. She had faith in their judgment, too.

She sighed, more content than she'd felt in a long time. Maybe ever.

A hand clamped around her arm, jerking her out of her reverie. Her eyes flew open and she tried to yank free, but the grip only tightened. Thomas's face was inches from hers. He was sitting next to her on the bench in a way that made it look like he'd just joined a friend.

"Found you," he sneered. "You've been a bad girl, Harley, running away from me and taking up with that guy. You're lucky I still love you." His hot breath blanketed her face as he spoke in a low, furious voice. "I'll take you back, but I'm going to make you pay for being with him. Are you sleeping with him? Don't worry, babe, I'll forgive even that once you've paid my price."

She froze. All the hope that had awakened in her lately disappeared, and she wanted to curl in on herself like she'd curled up on the floor when Thomas was beating her.

"Get up and walk away with me. Don't make a fuss, or it'll be worse for you."

In the past, she'd have done what he said, not wanting to call attention to herself. Now, though, she refused. She *wouldn't* go with him… but how could she get away?

"Now, Harley." Thomas started to rise, pulling her up with him. Her fingers tightened around the edge of the table, resisting.

As she opened her mouth to scream, Thomas's grip loosened. Garrett was on the other side of him, and his hand was clamped around Thomas's wrist.

"Let her go, or I'll snap your arm like a twig." Garrett's voice was quiet, but she'd never seen his face more serious. It gave her a glimpse of the man he must be when on a mission. Thomas's hand fell away from her.

"You've got no right to Harley," Thomas hissed. "She's mine."

"She doesn't belong to you or anyone else," Garrett said. "Stay away from her."

Thomas backed up a few feet, but he wasn't as cowed as he should be when facing a six-foot-three Navy SEAL. "Or what?"

Garrett didn't bother to answer. He just watched as Thomas retreated down the street and got in a car. Garrett turned to her then, the steeliness gone from his gaze. "Did he hurt you?" he asked, rubbing his hand over where Thomas's fingers had sunk into her arm.

She shook her head. Her arm would be bruised, but that was nothing in comparison to what would have happened if Thomas had gotten her somewhere private. "I want to go home," she whispered and began walking toward Garrett's truck. He fell in at her side. She could sense him keeping an eye on their surroundings, but she was focused on getting to the vehicle. He opened the passenger door for her. When she got in, she realized she was shaking, and a wave of nausea hit her.

"Take in deep breaths and let them out slowly, sweetheart. You're safe." He stayed with her, not touching her but keeping close by. "It's the adrenaline. It'll pass in a minute."

"You don't have that reaction?" she asked. He seemed perfectly calm.

"I'm used to dangerous situations." Of course he was. Scaring off one guy was nothing compared to what he usually did, she supposed.

"I didn't know what to do." That had scared her, too. Part of her had come close to complying because she simply hadn't been able to think of any other option.

"Yell, scream. Draw attention to yourself. I know that's not in your nature, but it's what you've got to do," he said. "People would have stepped in to help you. Most people are decent."

"Thomas is the exception to that." Fear was starting to be replaced by anger. "Damn him." Her life was headed in a good direction, but one encounter with Thomas threatened to suck her back down.

No. She wouldn't let it. She straightened, meeting Garrett's eyes for the first time since he rescued her. She saw concern there, and something else that she couldn't identify.

He blinked, and whatever it was disappeared. What had it been? Her own emotions were in too much turmoil to figure it out.

11

"This one is done. Ready for you, Violet." Imogen handed a curtain to Violet, who was ironing them after Imogen finished putting in the hems, while Mia was on a stepstool drilling holes in the wall. The women had shown up with their husbands and Matthew—and Imogen's sewing machine—that morning. The men were setting up the security system, and Imogen had insisted that she had plenty of extra fabric to make curtains for the bedrooms that hadn't been decorated yet.

Harley was in knots about the whole thing. These women were putting themselves out on her account, and she appreciated it, but she wasn't sure how to accept graciously. No one had ever done so much for her, even on the rare occasions when she'd asked for help.

"It's a good thing I love ironing," Violet quipped.

"I can do that," Harley quickly volunteered.

"No, seriously, I enjoy ironing, especially curtains. It's just long, steady strokes. It gives me time to think," Violet said. "Not like doing shirts with collars and cuffs."

"Do you iron Anderson's uniforms?" Harley asked.

"Guys in the service know how to iron, or they quickly learn," Violet explained. "Wrinkles during an inspection will get them in trouble."

"Oh, I didn't know." She was so ignorant about Garrett's life in the military.

"It's okay. There's a learning curve," Mia said from where she was hanging curtain rods. "They live by so many rules and regulations."

"Kenton more than anyone," Violet teased. "He's way more regimented than the other guys."

Mia laughed. "Yeah, that's true, but I'm working on loosening him up."

They continued to work and chat until the curtains were done and hung.

"I'm satisfied with these." Imogen surveyed their work with her hands on her hips. "And we've got time yet before we have to get the kids from the sitter."

"I brought treats." Mia pulled a pastry box from her bag. "We'll have a picnic and a little girl time." She plopped down on the rug and opened the box to reveal miniature cinnamon rolls and muffins. She'd even brought paper plates and napkins.

"I love a friend who works at a bakery." Violet sat and reached for a muffin. "Come on, you two."

Imogen immediately dropped to the floor to sit cross-legged, but Harley followed more cautiously. This having girlfriends thing was still new to her. After a brief discussion about the baked goods and an upcoming wedding that Mia was making the cake for, Imogen eyed Harley.

"Why don't you tell us about what happened yesterday?" she suggested. "You haven't brought it up, and I'm guessing you need to talk about it with someone other than a SEAL."

"I'm fine," Harley said. She'd kept her feelings inside since getting home, not wanting to dump them on Garrett. He was already so worried about getting the security system in place and protecting her physically. He shouldn't have to worry about her rattled state of mind, too.

"No, you're not. No one is fine after being accosted like that," Violet said, and Harley remembered that the woman was an analyst and had gone through her own share of frightening situations. "It's okay to talk about it."

Harley looked at the three faces around her. The women all wore encouraging looks. Maybe she could share, even though it felt awkward. "I don't know where to start."

"Wherever feels right," Mia encouraged.

"I guess I feel guilty because I completely let my guard down. I was just sitting there, soaking up the sunshine. I wasn't paying attention to anyone around me. I wasn't even looking." She'd had her eyes closed, for heaven's sake.

"There's nothing wrong with that. You deserve to be able to relax," Mia said.

Harley didn't know about that. She'd made poor choices in her life, her relationship with Thomas being the worst. "Anyway, Thomas was there before I knew it, sitting right next to me."

"Did he hurt you?" Imogen asked.

In answer, Harley pushed up her sleeve to reveal the bruises on her upper arm.

"Garrett couldn't have been happy about that," Mia observed.

"He wasn't." He hadn't said anything, but his eyes had stayed glued to the bruise when she was changing for bed the night before. He had wrapped his arms around her and held her all night. That had been comforting. Still, she wondered if she was making more bad decisions by being with him, by staying in this house.

"What else?" Violet prompted. "Did Thomas talk to you at all before Garrett scared him off?"

She repeated the threats Thomas had made and saw their eyes widen with surprise and sympathy.

"You poor thing. I'm so sorry you had to go through that," Mia said. "He sounds awful."

"One thing is for certain. That man made a mistake by coming after you." Imogen reached for Harley's hand and gripped it. "You're safe here."

"Am I?" That got right to the heart of all Harley's fears. She wasn't safe from Thomas. He'd gotten to her once, and she was convinced he could—and would—do so again. Garrett would protect her to the best of his ability, as would his friends, but they shouldn't have to. This was her problem, her mess to deal with. She didn't need to drag other people into it.

"Of course you are," Violet said. "The guys will get the security system in place, and nothing will get past Garrett. Remember, their job is to deal with threats and protect assets."

"I'm not an asset. I feel more like a liability. Maybe… maybe I should run. Take off and try to get away from Thomas that way." That had been in the back of her mind since the middle of a sleepless night. She didn't have much money, since Sebastian's accounts weren't available to her yet. She had enough to get few hundred miles, though, and if she used Sebastian's SUV, Thomas wouldn't recognize it.

The women shared a glance before Mia spoke. "Before you do anything like that, you have to talk with Garrett. Tell him how you're feeling and what you're thinking. He'll listen."

"I'm so sorry to have gotten him into this mess," Harley said. "It's not fair to him. He—"

"He's not going to see it that way," Violet assured her. "Talk to him. Today."

Harley knew they were right. She couldn't just take off on Garrett. That wouldn't be right, either. Before she could respond, Patrick appeared in the doorway.

"We're at a stopping point until we get the bandwidth expanded and get some other components we need," he announced before stooping to snag a cinnamon roll. He popped the treat in his mouth.

"We should get out of your hair," Mia said as they all stood. "But, Harley, please think about what we said, and call us if you need anything. We mean that—anything."

"Thanks," Harley said, still having a hard time believing that they were all so willing to help her. It seemed they were, though, and she had to admit that she needed people like them in her corner. "And thanks for the curtains."

"That's what friends do for each other." Imogen gave her a hug before joining Patrick, who had stepped into the hall.

A few minutes later, everyone was gone, and Harley went to find Garrett. He was in the den, sitting down with a laptop and his phone open to an app.

"Did it go well?" she asked. "Patrick said you still need some items."

"Yeah, we located them in Canfield, and he's gone after them. I'm still not totally satisfied with what we've got, though." His attention shifted from the laptop screen to the app. "It's not coming together the way it should."

"I'm sure it'll be fine."

"It has to be just right," he said. "Though nothing is going to function at a hundred percent until we get an upgrade on the bandwidth. I called the internet provider, but they can't get to it for a few days. In the meantime, I'm piecing as much of it together as I can, but I can't be sure—"

She touched his arm, stopping his words. Maybe this was the time to tell him that she was thinking of leaving Hartsville. Before she could speak, she felt him tense.

"What the hell does he think he's doing?" he asked, his eyes darkening as he put the laptop aside and stood. She looked at the screen. He must have installed a camera on the front of the house, because she saw the car Thomas had been driving approach.

Garrett was already headed toward the front door. She followed him as he stalked out. Thomas was standing at the bottom of the steps.

"Not one step closer," Garrett growled.

"Why not? I've got a legal right to be on property that my *wife* owns," Thomas said. "It's amazing what you can learn in a bar if you buy the locals a few drinks. So you're her dead brother's buddy, and she's inherited the house, property, money, even a boat. That's a sweet deal for her. And for me."

"None of it is yours," Garrett said.

"What's hers is mine." Thomas shifted his attention to Harley. She'd wrapped her arm around a post on the porch, needing to anchor herself against the fear going through her, but she wasn't going to cower in the house. "Come on, babe, we can have a sweet life here."

"No, Thomas." She managed to get the words out, even though her throat felt tight. "I don't want to see you ever again."

"You don't mean that." Thomas raised his foot as if to come up the stairs.

Garrett charged down them, sending Thomas stumbling back. "Get out of here. Now." Garrett didn't raise his voice, but his size and intensity had Thomas retreating toward his car.

"You're mine, Harley, and I'll have what's coming to me," Thomas called before getting in the vehicle. "But I can be patient while you get rid of this bozo. I'll be in touch." Thomas shot Garrett one last look.

As soon as he was out of sight, Harley sank down on the porch and pulled her knees up to her chin. She was never going to escape Thomas. All her dreams of living safely and happily in this house with her baby were unrealistic. Nothing in her life had worked out for the best. Why had she thought it could this time?

Garrett knelt in front of her. "Don't let him get to you."

"He'll always be able to get to me. Don't you see that? I think… I think I should leave. Go somewhere else until the divorce goes through and the judge has issued the restraining order. If I stay here, he'll keep coming back. I've got to go. It's the only way."

"Harley, don't think like that. This is your home."

"It may be my property, but I'm not safe here. Look how close he got. The security system might tell me he's there, but it won't stop him."

"It'll notify the police, once it's fully operational."

"And how long will it be before they come? Ten minutes? Twenty? In that amount of time, he could…" She didn't want to finish the thought. She hadn't been able to defend herself against Thomas in the past, and that wasn't going to change, especially as her pregnancy got further along. She was so vulnerable.

"If you leave, that's giving up."

"No," she argued, "it's surviving. Surviving is not giving up." She knew that firsthand. "And it's not just me. I have to protect the baby as well."

He shifted to sit next to her, and for a moment, there was only the sound of a bird in a nearby tree. That was her tree, darn it. She didn't want to leave her home, but she was afraid to stay.

"You're right," Garrett said. "I'm sorry. Believe me, nothing matters more to me than making sure you and your baby are safe. I get that you're scared, but I can protect you better here than on the run. And this *is* your home. You aren't going to feel safer in a motel somewhere."

He might be right about that. "I don't know. I just want this to be over." She wished she could see a time in her future when Thomas was no longer a threat, but she couldn't.

"Harley, you've got to trust me on this." Garrett found her hand and took it. "This is what I do. It's my area of expertise. I'll get the system running, and I will make sure you and the baby are protected. I promise you that. I won't leave you to deal with this on your own."

She did trust him. Once he committed to something, he'd see it through. Look at the work he'd done on the house. Protecting her from Thomas would be the same. And it was true that she didn't want him to go.

She did wish, though, that he heard her concerns more clearly. He didn't feel fear the way she did, and she had no words strong enough to convey her terror.

But he was right. Running wouldn't help. It would just mean looking over her shoulder in a different place, where she had no one to support her.

"All right," she finally said. "I'll stay."

"Good." He brought her knuckles to his lips and kissed them. "It'll be okay, sweetheart."

She wanted to believe that, but she'd faced too many disappointments in her life to share his confidence.

12

———————

"Harley," Garrett called as he climbed the stairs. He hadn't seen much of her during the day. They hadn't even connected at meals, since he'd worked straight through, fueled only by protein bars. Patrick and Matthew had returned to help him with the security system, and he'd wanted to maximize the time they'd been able to spare. The setup wasn't perfect yet, but it was a lot better than before. He'd keep working on it until it provided as much protection as possible.

As it was, he had cameras on all the corners of the house, plus others covering the doors and the first-floor windows. The doors and windows now had alarms that would sound if they were opened or broken. He wanted better night vision and faster access through the app, but that would come soon, when the last of the components were installed. He just needed to be patient, no matter how hard it was.

"In here," Harley said from the main bedroom. He'd been spending every night with her, but he still thought of the room as hers. She seemed to need her own space, a retreat of sorts, so he generally cleared out until bedtime.

He found her in one of the armchairs that flanked a large window. The curtains were drawn against the night, and she was curled up with her legs tucked under her and a book in her hands.

"Good book?" he asked, taking the opposite chair and studying her. Her skin was pale, with shadows under her eyes again, like when she'd first come. That had gotten better for a while, but now that Thomas had showed his nasty face, she seemed to be feeling the strain again. He'd do anything to take that burden from her. The security system should help, but until the situation with Thomas was resolved, she wouldn't be at peace.

"I don't know. I can't concentrate." She tossed the book onto the side table with a sigh. "I saw Thomas from the kitchen window today. He was walking along the edge of the lake. Not on my property, but close."

"The cameras picked him up." Garrett had watched him loiter in a public access area for almost an hour. Since he had no legal grounds to run him off, Garrett had just kept eyes on him.

"You knew?" Her voice rose. "Why didn't you tell me?"

"I didn't want you to worry. If he'd gotten any closer, I'd have dealt with it," he said, but her lips pinched shut. She clearly wasn't pleased with his response. "I'll do everything in my power to keep you safe, Harley."

"I don't feel safe," she insisted. "You don't know Thomas. He's mercurial. Right now, he's not being aggressive because he wants the inheritance Sebastian left me. He'll be nice, even charming, in hopes I'll cave. That's what he's waiting for."

"You're not considering going back to him, are you?" Garrett kept his tone mild, because she was entitled to make her own choices, but he hoped she understood that being with Thomas would be a huge mistake.

"I'm not." She hesitated, and he had the sense he wasn't going to like what was coming. "But I've been thinking that it might be better if I delay the divorce process until he's back in Florida. The lawyer called today, and I mentioned that Thomas was in town. It wouldn't take much to figure out where he's staying, so Mr. Burke suggested we have him served with the papers while he's here. He said it would avoid the complication of crossing state lines or something."

Garrett knew exactly where Thomas was staying. Anderson had ways of getting intel and had located Thomas at a motel on the edge of Hartsville.

"But I don't want to do that," she continued. "Once he's served and he knows that I'm really going through with the divorce, he'll be angry and unpredictable. It's better to wait, so he's not anywhere near me when he gets the papers."

"If that's what you want to do," Garrett said, trying to see it from her perspective. "But don't delay too long. You need the legal protection of having a divorce in progress to prevent him from approaching you or claiming any of your inheritance as his."

"I know. I'm just… He scares me. I've seen what he can do." A shudder went through her at what must have been terrible memories. Garrett wished he could erase them, but he knew that wasn't possible. What he could do was protect her now and make sure her future was secure.

"He won't ever touch you again. I won't let him. I promise you that," he said, wishing his words had the power to take her fear away.

"I need you," she whispered.

"You have me." That became more true each day he spent with her. He hoped she realized that. He rose, took her in his arms, and carried her to the bed. She was already wearing the oversized shirt she slept in, so he flipped back the covers and laid her down on the mattress.

He leaned down to kiss her sweet lips. When her arms went around his neck to hold him close, he almost got lost in her.

"Let me get undressed." He straightened reluctantly. Aware that she was watching him in the dim light of the reading lamp, he took his time removing his clothes, flexing his muscles and putting on a show. As he stripped off his T-shirt and jeans, her eyes were on him, drinking him in. She giggled when he made his pecs dance, and he grinned at her, wanting her to be happy. He turned his back to her as he lowered his boxers and stepped out of them, making sure he tightened his butt muscles.

"Nice ass," she said. "But I'd like to see the front."

"Yeah?" He looked at her over his shoulder. "How much?" He was rock hard, his dick jutting out.

She moved to the edge of the bed, so she was directly behind him. Her fingers lightly cupped his butt. "Turn around."

When he did, she stroked her hand up his length, starting at his balls and going to the tip of his erection. He sucked in a breath. It felt so damn good. Then she did it again. She leaned closer to swirl her tongue over the slit in his dick before taking him all the way into her mouth. She slowly drew back, grazing him with her teeth before sucking hard on the tip. God, it was amazing.

He couldn't take his eyes off her and what she was doing to him. It took all his self-control not to come in her mouth. He didn't want that, not when he hadn't taken care of her yet, so he touched her cheek, getting her attention. "Harley, you gotta stop."

"Can't take any more, sailor?" She grinned up at him, the shadows gone from her eyes.

"Not right now, but we can come back to that." He reached for her shirt and pulled it off over her head. He wanted to see all of her, wanted to caress every inch of her body.

Once he joined her in bed, he started at her thighs, placing kisses on the delicate skin there. He slowly worked his way up, running his lips over her hip bones and around her navel. She lifted up, letting her legs fall farther apart, silently telling him what she wanted. He was eager to comply, running his tongue up her slit and taking her clit into his mouth. She was so wet for him, so hot. He'd never been more turned on, tasting her, feeling her responses, knowing that she wanted him. He continued loving her, listening to her gasps of pleasure, until he felt a tug on his hair.

"Stop," she whispered. "I want to ride you."

No man ever argued with that sentence, so he rolled onto his back. He had to bite the inside of his cheek to keep from coming immediately when she straddled him and rolled a condom onto his dick.

"I'm not going to last long, sweetheart," he said.

She came down on him in one move, robbing him of any brain power he had left. "Neither am I, but we're going to do this together." She squeezed her inner muscles around him and began to move. Her hands were braced against his chest as she lifted and lowered herself. Her breasts swayed, the nipples hard. They called out to him, so he rose up to take first one, then the other in his mouth.

His hands were on her hips, supporting and guiding her. He couldn't say which of them came first, but it didn't matter as they rode their orgasms to a finish together. She collapsed onto his chest, both of them breathing hard. He wrapped his arms around her and held her tight, loving everything about that moment.

Eventually, she rolled off him. He got up to dispose of the condom, but when he returned, she snuggled in close to him. They were quiet for a long time, and he'd thought she'd fallen asleep, when she spoke.

"Does it matter to you if I delay the divorce? I mean, does it matter between us?"

The switch back to that topic surprised him, but he didn't have any problem answering. "The timing of your divorce won't change how I feel about you." Her divorce was a formality, nothing more than that. He wanted to be with her. That was all he knew.

She was silent for a long time. "Okay, then," she finally said. "I'm going to wait a little while on it."

He didn't love her choice, but he could live with it so long as he was with her. The restraining order was a different story, though. He didn't want to bring it up now, but he felt he had to. "You still need the restraining order, so you've got legal recourse if Thomas approaches you again."

She sighed. "Mr. Burke said it's always slow getting those in place, especially since I never called the police on Thomas in the past. No paper trail. He said he's working on it."

"That's good," Garrett said, though he couldn't help feeling it wasn't good enough. Not nearly. He needed to find a way to expedite that process. As he thought about how, he stroked her back, something that always soothed her. Once she was asleep, he slipped out of bed.

Downstairs, he first ran diagnostics on the security system to make sure it was functioning properly. When he was satisfied it was, he switched his attention to the files Harley had shared with him containing Thomas's voicemails and texts. He went through them again. Most were from the past few weeks, but she'd kept some older ones as well, which helped to establish a history of harassment, if not abuse. He called Kenton, figuring he would know the community and local authorities best.

"If I want to fast-track the restraining order against Thomas, who do I call?" Garrett asked.

"Did something happen? Has he come at Harley again? I can be there in ten minutes if you need me."

"No, nothing new. I just can't wait around any longer. Harley's scared, and I can't stand seeing her that way."

"I get that. Judge Darrow is your best bet. She's a friend of my parents. Give me a few minutes and I'll get her contact information for you from my mom. I'll text it," Kenton said. "Tell Harley we're all looking out for her. She'll be okay."

"I keep trying to convince her," Garrett said, "but she's not used to having people help her."

"Give her time."

"Yeah. Thanks, man." Time was something Garrett didn't have much of. His date to report to base was drawing closer, and he had to do everything in his power for Harley before that.

When Kenton sent Judge Darrow's email address and phone number, Garrett barely hesitated before forwarding the file of Thomas's threats. He knew he might be overstepping, but he had to make sure Harley was safe. The restraining order was a necessary step in the process. Harley would understand that. She had to.

13

Garrett eased the den door closed after giving Harley a morning kiss and dropping off a protein shake for her to sip while on her daily Zoom. She had a big project due at the end of the day and had told him she'd be busy. That was okay with him, since he had a few projects to finish up before deploying.

And it was a potential deployment after all.

He walked back to the kitchen and cleaned up from breakfast, thinking about the email he'd received that morning. His team had been put on standby for an overseas assignment.

Normally, he'd be riding a wave of adrenaline and excitement about getting back out there, doing an important job he was trained for and had sworn to do. Everything was different this time, though. He'd wanted to ease into his separation from Harley by returning on weekends to be with her.

He hadn't told her about the possible deployment, because he wasn't sure how she'd take it. Their relationship was still new, and they had yet to have a serious conversation about their future. Still, he couldn't dismiss the feeling that he was truly alive every moment he spent with her—perhaps even more than when he was on a mission with his team. That didn't make much sense in his rational brain. Maybe it didn't have to.

He did know he couldn't leave her without making sure the house was completely safe for her and the coming baby. So he'd texted Patrick earlier, asking for assistance with a wiring issue. He and Sebastian had deemed the house's older wiring acceptable for the time being, but he didn't want Harley to have any problems when he wasn't around to fix them.

He heard Patrick's truck pull up and walked out to greet him, disengaging the alarm on the keypad by the front door. "Hey, man. Thanks for coming."

"No worries," Patrick said. "Something malfunctioning?"

Garrett shook his head and stepped out onto the porch. "Just some things I want to deal with." He lowered his voice, not that he thought Harley could hear him. "I might be on an overseas deployment sooner than expected. I gotta make sure the house is ready for Harley and the baby."

"Got it." Of course Patrick would understand that need. He left Imogen and their kids on missions that could last for months. Before they could go inside, a delivery van pulled into the driveway. "You order something?" Like Garrett, Patrick was always cautious.

"Yeah, some stuff for the baby." Garrett ignored Patrick's raised eyebrow and took the large box from the driver.

"What kind of stuff?" Patrick asked, following him into the house.

"Babyproofing." After reading about what was necessary and checking the online reviews, he'd placed an order for various products. "I can't predict when I'll be back if I go overseas, and I don't want Harley to have to worry about any of this." He put the box on the kitchen table and slit it open.

"Damn." Patrick was looking over Garrett's shoulder. "You plan to install all that today *and* fix the electrical?"

"Hope to." There was no time to waste, given that he could get called to base at any time. Ever since he'd read that email, he'd felt like a stopwatch was ticking in his head.

"We're going to need help." Patrick pulled out his phone and sent a group text message, asking their fellow SEALs to come over. Replies came in quickly. "Reinforcements are on the way. Let's get started with the wiring."

The two of them worked in the attic and basement, running new wire to update the electrical in those areas so it would be less likely to trip a breaker. When the other guys arrived, they worked their way through the house installing electrical outlet covers, gates on the stairs, and cabinet locks.

"Are you sure you want me to put this on?" Matthew held up a toilet seat lock. He had insisted on helping, even if the tasks he could do were limited by his still-healing hand. "I mean, the kid's barely a bump at this point. That's a long way from playing in the toilet."

Patrick, Kenton, and Anderson shared a look, but they didn't speak.

"Yeah, I'm sure. I don't want Harley to have to do anything later on. She's got enough to worry about." Another look got exchanged. "What?" Garrett demanded.

"We get it, man," Kenton said. "I went a little nuts when I came home and found Mia and the girls living in my house. They were toddlers at the time, and she hadn't childproofed because… because she's Mia." That got a chuckle from everyone. Mia had a reputation for approaching life differently. She was of the belief that if you discouraged children from opening cabinets or sticking their fingers into outlets, they wouldn't. Kenton grinned. "Needless to say, I couldn't live like that, so we compromised. Which leads me to ask, have you talked to Harley about this?"

"My time's limited, and I needed to make decisions," Garrett said. He felt an even greater sense of urgency than he had a few days earlier when he'd ordered the supplies. "I think she'll be happy about it."

"We'll go with that," Patrick said. "I'll help you with the bathroom stuff, Matthew." As the two of them went into the downstairs powder room, Garrett heard Patrick say, "Just roll with it, dude. You'd understand if you were in Garrett's shoes. Leaving when you've got someone depending on you is tough."

It sure was. It might not be so bad if Harley weren't in danger from an abusive husband. But Garrett had the feeling he'd be worked up about being deployed even without that. Leaving her was going to be hell.

"What the heck?" Harley stood in the bathroom, staring at some sort of mechanism on the toilet that hadn't been there that morning. "What is this thing?" She fiddled with it, trying to get the lid up.

She'd been working for hours and had just finished her project. Her big reward for that was a trip to the bathroom and maybe a snack. She pushed the button on the top again and yanked on the strap holding the seat down. Nothing. What kind of craziness was this, to prevent a pregnant woman from peeing?

Maybe the toilets upstairs didn't have similar contraptions. She was about to head up there when she saw a man moving on the front porch. Her breath caught in her throat before she recognized Matthew. She marched to the door and opened it, hoping he knew the secret to getting the toilet lid up.

"Hey, Harley," he said.

"What is that thing on the toilet?" she asked. She had to pee too badly to waste time with niceties.

"It's a safety lock. It prevents the lid from being opened," he answered.

Yeah, she got that, but why in the world was it on her toilet? "Do you know how to work it? I tried the button on top."

"The button's a decoy, according to the package," Matthew explained. "You've got to pinch in on both sides to release the mechanism."

"Good to know." She dashed back to the bathroom and did as he'd said. Sure enough, it worked, and just in time. Her need to pee was probably going to get worse over the coming months. No way was she dealing with toilet locks when they weren't necessary.

She came out of the bathroom to find Matthew pacing in the foyer. She had a thing or two to say to Garrett about babyproofing when her delivery date was months out, but she wouldn't take it out on Matthew. Poor guy didn't deserve that. He was battling his own set of challenges.

"Sorry about that," he said, as if it were his fault.

"It's okay. Is Garrett around?" The house seemed empty except for Matthew.

"He and the other guys went to grab some dinner."

"And you got left on guard duty?" she guessed.

"Something like that. I don't mind. It's nice here. Peaceful."

"I do love the front porch," she agreed. She could see herself spending hours on it as the weather got warmer. The back deck overlooked the lake, and that would be a great spot to relax, too. She reminded herself that she was lucky to be here and have this, even if she had problems to deal with.

"How's your hand? Is it hurting less?" She wasn't sure she should ask about it, but it felt rude not to. Garrett had told her some about how the injury had occurred. Like her brother, Matthew had been trying to save innocent people. He deserved her respect, and she liked him. Despite his injury, he was positive and kind.

He shrugged. "Getting there."

Harley wasn't sure that was true, but she let it go. She wasn't going to force him to talk about it. She looked out the window alongside the front door and tensed when she saw a car turning in off the street.

"That's Mia," Matthew said. They walked out onto the porch together.

When Mia got out of her car and pulled a pastry box and a thermos from her back seat, Harley felt again how fortunate she was to have not only the house but a group of friends who looked out for her. She had Sebastian—and Garrett—to thank for that.

"Hi," Mia called. "I brought treats."

"You'll spoil me," Harley said with a smile, "but thanks."

"I can't stand for things to get thrown away at the end of the day. We donate leftovers to the local food pantry if there's enough. Today, there were only a few items." She set the thermos down on the steps and opened the box so Matthew could choose a treat.

"Won't your girls want those?" Matthew asked.

"I bake with them all the time," Mia said. "Trust me, they get plenty of sweets. Please help yourself."

"Thanks." Matthew took a large cookie. "I'm going to take a walk down by the lake. Yell if you need me."

"He's a good one," Mia commented when Matthew had gone around the corner of the house.

"They all are." Harley invited Mia in and led the way to the kitchen.

"True. Awesome men," Mia said. "Kenton is not the kind of guy I ever saw myself being with, but love is love."

"Not your usual type?" Harley got plates and mugs from the cabinet, and they sat down at the table.

Mia laughed. "Not at all. He's far too regimented, and he says I'm too chaotic. We meet somewhere in the middle, though, when it matters. We're good for each other that way."

"It can't be easy," Harley said. "I mean, how do you manage when he's gone for long stretches?" That had been bothering her, and Mia was someone she could ask about it.

Mia put a couple of cookies on Harley's plate and poured out the rich coffee—"Don't worry; it's decaf"—before answering. "Well, there's the good, the bad, and the ugly. Which do you want first?"

"The ugly." Harley had a lifetime of experience in dealing with the worst-case scenario. She always wanted to get that out in the open first.

"Okay. For me, the ugliest is dealing with how much Emma and Ava miss him. At first, I can talk up the girl time we get, but that only works for so long. After he's been gone a while, they can be inconsolable at times. Once they're older, I hope they'll understand better. At the age they are now, that's impossible. It breaks my heart to see how much they miss him."

Harley could imagine how difficult that would be. At least the girls weren't yet aware how much danger Kenton was in when he was deployed. "So… the bad, then?"

"Everything else," Mia sighed. "Going to bed alone, waking up alone, no kisses in the backyard, long evenings by myself after the girls are asleep. I miss him every day when he's gone. His voice, his smile." Mia got a faraway look on her face for a moment. "And then there's managing everything. If the car breaks down or the sink backs up, he's not there to help. I have to deal with whatever. His parents are great—all I have to do is call them—but it's not the same." She took a sip of coffee, pausing for a moment before going on. "There's no one to make decisions with. That was one of the things that surprised me after we got together. I'd lived alone for years, taken in the girls on my own, and thought I was fine. But after being with Kenton, I found I didn't want that anymore. We're a couple, a partnership. It's just that sometimes we're on opposite sides of the globe."

Like Mia, Harley was used to being alone, but she'd started to rely on Garrett more and more in the short time she'd known him. She had serious concerns about how she'd go on when he left, and not just because she needed his protection. It was him. She wanted him around… or just plain wanted him… more than she would have thought possible. Sure, he went overboard sometimes, like with the babyproofing, but his heart had been in the right place.

"So what's the good part of being with a SEAL?" she asked.

Mia's smile flashed wide. "When he walks in the door after a mission. It's like falling in love all over again. The girls dash for him first. After they get their hugs and kisses, it's my turn. And I don't let go quickly. The first night when he's back is… magical."

Nights with Garrett were already that way. Harley couldn't imagine how good it would be after a separation. So that was everything: the good, the bad, and the ugly, but she had to ask. "Does the good outweigh the bad and the ugly?"

"It has to," Mia answered with a lift of her shoulders, "because I can't give him up. That's unfathomable, so we make it work. Do I sometimes wish he worked a job that allowed him to be home every evening? Of course I do, but being a SEAL is an integral part of him. I can't ask him to change."

Harley understood that, since the same seemed to be true for Garrett. She appreciated Mia's honesty, but she had to wonder if she could deal with it as well as Mia, Imogen, and Violet did. It couldn't be easy on them or their relationships. Despite that, the couples appeared happy.

The question was whether she had what it took to be with a SEAL. Though maybe she was getting ahead of herself by even worrying about it. Garrett hadn't said anything about continuing their relationship beyond the upcoming weekends when he planned to visit her.

Still, their connection felt special, worlds apart from anything she'd ever experienced. She'd always longed for a true connection with a man, a relationship in which she was loved and valued, and she could envision that growing with Garrett. Despite all the challenges being with a SEAL would pose, she couldn't help hoping that they could have so much more than a short-term fling.

14

———————

Harley punched in the code on the security keypad so that she could walk out onto the porch. She'd just finished her work for the day and wanted to be outside. The spring weather she could see from the den window had been calling to her throughout the afternoon. She needed a walk, needed to stretch her legs and feel the warmth of the sunshine.

A lap around the house and maybe a few minutes down by the lake would do it for her. She made it to the bottom of the porch steps before she heard the house door open behind her and sighed. Over the past two days, Garrett had been adamant about her staying indoors. As much as she loved her home, she was starting to feel trapped.

"Where are you going?" he asked.

"For a walk. I need to get out of the house," she said, continuing on her way.

"Harley, wait." She could hear him hurrying across the newly repaired porch. "If you're going, I have to be with you. You can't be outside alone."

She spun around, suddenly irritated with him. She got that he was only trying to protect her, but still. "Seriously? I just need a minute, and Thomas hasn't made an appearance in four days." In the time since she'd seen him near the lake, her fear of him had begun diminishing. "He must have gone back to Florida. He does have to work, you know." Thomas was a stickler about going to his jobs.

Garrett winced. "Yeah, about that." He rubbed the back of his neck.

"What?" She didn't have patience for him to play games right now.

"I asked Anderson to do some digging into Thomas, and what he found… it's not good. I'm guessing you didn't know that he works for a crime syndicate."

"What?" She shook her head. "He sells used cars during the day and is a bouncer at a club a few nights a week." Thomas had always been secretive, but organized crime? That was ridiculous.

"The car salesman gig is legit, but the club he bounces for is owned by the mob," Garrett explained. "Thomas owes them a substantial gambling debt, and if he doesn't work it off… well, let's just say that his employers aren't nice people."

"I can't believe that." She'd been to the club, and Thomas's boss had been friendly to her. It had seemed like a perfectly normal place. "And even if that were true, wouldn't it be more reason for him to get home so he can work?"

"It *is* true. He apparently placed big bets on sports, particularly football."

That part *did* make some sense. Thomas never missed watching a game and tended to react strongly to wins and losses. She rubbed her left arm. During one game, when his favorite team had been losing, he'd twisted her arm behind her when she'd asked him to turn the volume down.

"The thing is, Thomas may be even more desperate than we thought. He wants your inheritance, Harley."

"How long have you known about this?"

"Couple of days," he admitted, which coincided with his increased vigilance.

"You might have told me." She crossed her arms over her chest.

"I didn't want to upset you."

That had backfired. It was bad enough to find out her husband was a gambler, but she'd already known Thomas was garbage. Now Garrett —who she'd trusted—had made a choice about what she was and wasn't allowed to know. It felt infantilizing and controlling. Anger rose in her as she stared at him.

Had she made the same mistake again and trusted the wrong man?

"I'm sorry," Garrett said. "But you've got to see why it's so important that you stay in the house—or, if you go out, to have me with you. To protect you."

"You'll be leaving soon, though," she said. He'd told her that his coming assignment could take him overseas, potentially for months. No weekend visits, like they'd talked about. She'd be here alone. All the time.

Despite her anger, that scared her—which irritated her even more. She'd spent most of the past year being frightened, and she was tired of it.

"I know. I wish… The security system will help." He paused, and a fleeting guilty look crossed his face.

"I can't be a prisoner in the house forever," she said. "I can't, Garrett. You have to see that."

"Sweetheart—"

"I want to be safe. I want my baby to be safe. But I can't stay in the house twenty-four seven until… until when? When will this end?" She couldn't see a good outcome to the situation. Was she going to be in limbo forever, waiting for Thomas to come after her? He'd already taken too much of her life.

The only conclusion she could reach was that, without Garrett's protection, she couldn't stay here. She'd pushed aside the idea of leaving days ago, but her need to run was back, stronger than ever. Going somewhere Thomas couldn't find her felt like the only option. Once she had access to Sebastian's bank accounts, she could take off. Make a new life for herself elsewhere.

"I don't know," Garrett said. "I—"

"I'm leaving," she declared, cutting him off. "I can't be here any longer. I'm going to find a place where I'm safe and stay there. I'll be more cautious this time and not leave a trail for Thomas to find." She was thinking aloud. "There must be a way to disappear."

People did. They moved across the country and started over. She could do that. Maybe a city on the West Coast, where no one would notice someone new. She'd quit her job and find another. Her skills and experience were transferable.

"You can't do that," Garrett said.

"Why? What's more important than me and the baby being safe?" Did Garrett have some personal reason he wanted her to stay? They'd forged a connection, even built a relationship of sorts, but neither of them had taken the next step to suggest it might be something more.

"You own a home here." He gestured behind him, and her hopes deflated like a popped balloon. He'd had the perfect opportunity to say how he felt about her, and he'd bypassed it to make a logical argument. "You have friends. People who care about you."

She had the SEALs and their wives. They'd invited her into their circle.

"Besides, I thought you liked Hartsville," he continued.

I like being with you, she wanted to shout, but he was carefully keeping this not about them, so she didn't feel comfortable bringing that element up.

"I do," she said after a minute. "It's a great place, and I can see why Sebastian chose to make his home here, but I can't live in fear." The sense of community *was* wonderful, but it didn't outweigh the threat.

"Running won't fix this. No matter where you go, you'll be looking over your shoulder," he warned.

She saw the logic of his argument, but, dammit, didn't he understand that she was terrified? Staying in Hartsville was unthinkable if Thomas wasn't dealt with.

"I'm a sitting duck here. Don't you understand that? You probably aren't scared of anything. Why would you be?" Garrett's training and size made him seem impervious. "After you're gone, when I need to go to the grocery store or a doctor's appointment, how will I be safe? I can't protect myself against Thomas. I tried when he first started abusing me. Then I gave up."

She saw the anguish on Garrett's face, and she appreciated that he cared about what she'd been through. Even so, she wanted to fold in on herself, to give in to the fear she felt. She couldn't do that, though. It wasn't just about her anymore. She had a baby to protect. A little life to love.

There was no choice, as she saw it. She had to leave Hartsville. She was about to say that when her phone rang. She glanced at the screen, determined not to answer if the number was unknown. She couldn't take hearing Thomas's voice right then. It would break her.

But the caller ID showed the Hartsville police station, so she accepted the call. "Hello."

"Good afternoon, I'm Officer Beckwith with the Hartsville PD. Is this Harley Von?"

"Yes." Could Thomas possibly be in jail? It would be just like him to have her be his phone call.

"I'm calling to inform you that the judge has approved your restraining order. It's in effect as of today, and Thomas Von has been notified of the consequences should he approach you."

"The restraining order?" she asked, her eyes on Garrett's face. That guilty look she'd seen earlier reappeared.

"Yes, ma'am," the officer said. "We'll make sure extra patrols go past your house. If you see any sign of Mr. Von, call 9-1-1 immediately. That's important. A lot of people in these circumstances—I mean, when it's family—hesitate to call the authorities because they believe they can reason with the person. That's never a good idea."

"I understand. Thank you for the advice." She hung up and turned on Garrett. "You did this, didn't you? You pushed it through."

"I had to, Harley," he said. "It had to be done, so I sent your voice-mails to the judge."

Her world crumbled at his words. She'd trusted him to respect her wishes to wait. Garrett had acted anyway, with no regard for her opinion, and hadn't even told her. Because he was so sure he knew best.

"Thomas will be furious now. I told you that. I thought you understood," she said. Her voice cracked, betraying her emotions, but she kept going. "You've made the situation worse."

"Harley, the restraining order is the best way to protect you after I'm gone." His tone was pacifying, as though he were talking to a child. "I couldn't leave here without knowing you had the legal protection it provides."

"That was *my* choice to make."

"I'm not arguing that, and I'm sorry I upset you, but I had to take action. I had to." He took a step closer. "Harley, I'd do anything to keep you safe. You have to know that I can't stand the thought of something happening to you. That would kill me. I won't risk your life—or let you risk it."

"But you'll keep me 'safe' by making decisions for me," she argued. Part of her wanted to give in, let Garrett hold her, curl into his strength. She refused, forcing herself to stand strong. "You violated my trust, took advantage of information I shared with you. That's the worst thing you could have done to me. You know what I've been through. The choices you made…" She shook her head, afraid of what she was about to say but knowing she had to say it anyway. "Those choices make me question what's between us."

She recognized that his motives were good. They came from the heart… but that wasn't justification enough. Not anymore. Being with Garrett and seeing his friends' marriages had changed her perspective. For the first time in her life, she understood what it meant to be in a loving, equitable relationship, and she didn't want one where she wasn't respected. She had to pull back, end things before she fell for him any more.

"You should go," she said, drawing on all her resolve to get the words out.

His brows rose in surprise. "Harley, that's not wise. I can't leave you like this."

"It's my house, Garrett. My house, and I'll make the decisions. Get your stuff and go. Please." If he argued with her, she'd waver, so she needed this to be over quickly. "Now."

He moved his hands as if he were going to reach for her, but she walked around him and up the steps onto the porch.

"Can we talk about this? Please." His hands were on his hips, and he was looking up at her.

"Did *we* talk about handing over my personal files to a judge?"

He dropped his head before going past her into the house. Through the open door, she watched him go up the stairs. She waited on the porch for him to return. When he did, a few minutes later, he dropped his duffel bag at his feet and faced her.

"Please promise me that you won't take off," he said, surprising her. She'd expected him to make a pitch to stay, maybe even confess he loved her. Neither of those things seemed to be on his agenda. "Thomas tracked you down once, and he can do it again. It's more difficult to disappear than people imagine."

He was probably right about that, she silently conceded. The idea of running still held some appeal, but she'd give him this one thing. At least for now. "I promise."

"And set the alarm."

"I don't promise to stay in the house forever." She wasn't going to be a prisoner, no matter how frightened she was.

"Just arm the system, and keep it that way when you're inside." His expression was pleading, so she nodded. "Goodbye, Harley."

She opened her mouth, but nothing came out as her emotions hit her. She was forcing a man she cared deeply about to leave her. Before the tears could hit, she rushed inside and closed the door. She punched in the numbers on the keypad, keeping her promise. She risked one glance out the window alongside the door. Garrett stood there with his phone in his hand, looking at the screen. No doubt he was checking the app that would tell him the security system was engaged.

After a moment, he got in his truck and drove off. Harley staggered into the living room and collapsed on the sofa.

15

———————

Harley's tears flowed freely as she sobbed into a sofa pillow, feeling betrayed and abandoned. Maybe she was overreacting, but between the pregnancy, the threat from Thomas, and Garrett leaving, she couldn't stop crying.

After several minutes, she forced herself to sit up and reached for a tissue. She wiped at her eyes, but the tears kept coming. It didn't help that her sobs seemed to echo in the room. Without Garrett, the house felt empty and far too large for her. All of it compounded the bone-deep loneliness that she'd dealt with ever since her mother's death.

She swallowed down the next sob, struggling to right herself. She wasn't as alone as she'd been at other times in her life. She could call a friend. Her connection with the SEALs and their wives might have begun because of Garrett, but she felt that they *were* her friends.

She debated for only a minute before reaching for her phone and calling Imogen. Since she taught kindergarten, she should be home by this time of day, and she was so kind and nurturing.

"Hi, Harley," Imogen answered on the first ring. "I was just going to call to invite you and Garrett to dinner. I'm making lasagna, and—"

"I can't," Harley broke in. "Garrett's left, and I…" Renewed sobs prevented her from going on.

"Oh, honey, what happened?"

Harley told her about Garrett's hypervigilance and how he'd pushed through the restraining order behind her back, taking the decision out of her hands. She had to stop several times to compose herself before she got it all out.

"I can understand your reaction, but that's how SEALs are wired," Imogen said when Harley was done. "I'm not saying he was right, but Garrett is who he is. He takes care of the people who are important to him."

"Does that mean me?" Harley could barely whisper the question. That was at the heart of all this. If he cared for her, she couldn't understand how he'd act without consulting her, even if it was in her best interests. He knew how little control she'd had over her life, and she'd thought he understood how that had impacted her.

"Of course it does."

"He's never said so." Harley had been waiting for some kind of declaration, but it hadn't come.

"They don't. Trust me on this. Words can be hard for the warrior types, but he's shown you, hasn't he?" Imogen asked gently.

He had, Harley admitted. He'd shown her in the way he worked on the house, trying to get everything possible done before he had to leave. In the way his every thought was to protect her. Not to mention a thousand little things, like making food that appealed to her or running a bath for her. And the way he held her at night spoke volumes. Yes, he'd shown her in his way.

"I guess." Her tears slowed and she took in a full breath, feeling her body and emotions settling a bit.

"Okay, then. The question is—"

The sound of breaking glass made Harley leap off the sofa. She dropped her phone and watched it slide under the coffee table, but she didn't move to retrieve it. Her attention was riveted by the sight of Thomas stepping through the smashed dining room window and coming into the room. He held a knife in his hand. She felt sick.

"Thomas," she gasped.

"Found you, babe." He was smiling in a way she'd learned not to trust. "So stupid of you to think I wouldn't get to you. I just had to wait for your guard dog to leave."

"You need to go." She found her voice, even if it was shaking. "I have a restraining order against you, so you can't be here."

Thomas chuckled and pulled a crumpled sheet of paper from his pocket. "The police gave me a copy." He wadded it up and tossed it over his shoulder. "That doesn't mean a damn thing. You know what does, babe?" When she didn't answer, he stepped closer to her. "Inheritance laws. I've been studying up on those. When there's no will, the spouse gets everything."

She moved backward, but her legs bumped into the coffee table. The feel of the wood against her calves reminded her that her phone was under there. Could Imogen hear what was happening? Was she listening in and getting help? If so, Harley had to buy herself some time. She had to keep Thomas talking. "I don't understand what you mean, Thomas." She raised her voice as she spoke, to be heard better through the phone.

"It's simple. When you're dead, I'll get it all." He gestured around him. "This house, your brother's money—hell, even the boat. That's pretty damn sweet."

Oh God. He was going to kill her. That was his plan. Kill her and get what was hers. And she was trapped in the room with him. She couldn't escape. He was quick, and he was stronger than she was. She knew that from experience. Worse, he was ruthless.

"I'll give you whatever you want. Money. Whatever. Just go away." The last thing she wanted to do was let him have anything that had been Sebastian's. She wanted to tell him to go to hell. That none of it was his, and it never would be. But provoking him would just make him strike. She needed to keep him calm.

"No way. I checked on the value of this house. It's worth a pretty penny. Probably even more now, since your boyfriend has put so much work into it. It, along with the money, is my golden ticket."

"To pay off your gambling debts?" She shouldn't bait him, but something in her wanted him to know she'd found that out. He'd held all the power between them in the past, but no more.

He narrowed his eyes and brandished the knife at her. "How do you know about those?"

She shrugged, trying to look casual, but she was on her guard for the moment when he'd come at her. He was playing with her now, keeping a few feet between them. He'd always enjoyed doing that before he abused her. "Something I heard."

"From that SEAL. He thinks he's something. I'd like to take a stab at him, too. Think I will, after I'm done with you." Thomas took another step toward her, keeping the knife held in front of him. "I'll be quick if you don't fight me."

"Thomas, think about this." Her knees were quaking, but she held her ground. "You won't get away with it. There's security on the house—

cameras showing you're here. It's broad daylight, for goodness' sake. The police are probably on their way already." At least, she was praying they were, praying that Imogen had called for help.

She saw a kind of madness in his eyes that she'd only glimpsed once before—the day after her birthday when he'd physically and verbally abused her so horrifically. Thomas was beyond reasoning with, but she had to make one last effort. So she said the only thing she could think of that might slow him down.

"I'm pregnant with your baby," she blurted out.

"Nice try," he snarled, "but you know I used protection." Early in their marriage, he'd promised her that children would come later, claiming that he wanted it to be just the two of them to start with.

"Not always. We didn't on my birthday," she reminded him. They hadn't had sex for at least two months before that night, but Thomas had turned on the charm for the celebration. He'd been the man she'd thought he was when they first got together. He'd taken her out to a fancy dinner and given her a beautiful necklace. Briefly, foolishly, she'd hoped that he'd changed and that their marriage could be a good one.

The next day, though, the nightmare had begun again. He'd hit her and torn through the house, turning over furniture and emptying the contents of the kitchen cabinets onto the floor. He'd made her clean it all up to show her gratitude to him for the gift. That had been the day she decided she had to escape—but it was only when Sebastian contacted her that she saw a way of making that plan a reality.

"Oh, yeah, you're right about that. So you're knocked up?" The malicious smirk she'd learned to fear was on his face. "It's funny you'd think I'd care about some kid nobody can even see yet."

Garrett had cared. She bit her tongue to keep from saying it. He'd babyproofed the entire house, even if it hadn't been necessary.

"It's your child," she said instead. "Doesn't that mean anything to you?"

It didn't. He'd made that clear, but talking about the baby had gained her a few minutes and added to her resolve. She had to protect her child. She needed to run. Could she sprint away from him and make it out the back of the house? If she did, where would she go?

Thomas must have seen her glance toward the open den door, because he moved in quickly and grabbed her by her hair. "I think the baby goes first."

She screamed as he pointed the knife at her stomach.

After leaving Harley's place, Garrett drove the short distance to Patrick and Imogen's house and pulled into their driveway. He sat for a few minutes with his hands still gripping the wheel.

Why the hell had he walked away? Harley had the right to order him out of her house—he would never override that, never want her to feel that her home wasn't hers to manage—but he could have parked down the driveway to keep an eye on things. Recon was a familiar role, and he'd put up with a hell of a lot more than an uncomfortable, sleepless night in his truck if it meant keeping Harley safe.

But now that he was here, he felt a powerful urge to talk things through with his friend. Maybe Patrick would have some advice on how he could fix this. Garrett knew enough of the story behind Patrick and Imogen's early relationship to believe that Patrick would have some useful insight to share.

"What's up?" Patrick asked.

"Harley kicked me out," Garrett blurted.

Patrick put down the hand planer he'd been using on a piece of wood. "Why?"

"I submitted the evidence for the restraining order without telling her."

"Shit, dude. Women don't like it when you overstep."

"I had to," Garrett protested. "What's going to happen when I get deployed? Who'd protect her if the police weren't already on the alert?"

"I'm right down the road."

"You can't guarantee you'll be around, either. You could get deployed, too." So could all his SEAL buddies in the area. He had to be able to rely on the local police. He feared they wouldn't respond quickly enough to keep her from getting scared or even bruised again, like she'd been the other day, but at least he wanted them to put Thomas in jail if he came at Harley. The restraining order was the best hope of that.

"That's true," Patrick agreed. "What's the solution, though? We can't simply go after Thomas and eliminate the threat."

"Exactly. Until he makes a move, I can't do anything." The law, not to mention his superior officers, wouldn't be pleased if Garrett threatened or attacked Thomas without direct provocation. It was excruciating. Harley had said she was a sitting duck, and Garrett felt like he was sitting on his hands when all he wanted to do was act.

"Let's think this through," Patrick said. "Maybe Harley would agree to stay here with us, or with Kenton or Anderson. That way she wouldn't be alone."

"Still a short-term fix." And contingent on convincing Harley to do it. She'd been ready to run from town to escape Thomas, but would she consider staying with their friends? Possibly. "It's worth a try, though."

"Let's go talk to Imogen and get her opinion." Patrick led the way into the kitchen, where Imogen was leaning against the counter, talking on the phone. When she saw them, she pointed to the phone and mouthed, "Harley."

Garrett felt relieved that Harley had reached out to a friend. Maybe she'd be willing to speak with him and give him a chance to apologize. He was just about to ask to talk with Harley when a notification from the security app sounded on his phone. At the same moment, Imogen's eyes went wide.

"Oh my God. He's there," Imogen whispered.

"Thomas?" Patrick asked as his wife muted her end of the call and put the phone on speaker. Faint voices came through.

Garrett opened the app and scanned the intel. The dining room window, facing onto the porch, had been smashed, giving Thomas access to the house. Garrett switched to the interior camera view of the downstairs and saw Thomas in the living room with Harley. He had a knife, but, thank God, he was still several feet away from her.

Garrett was headed for the door when Patrick grabbed his arm.

"I've gotta roll," he said, shaking off the hold. Harley needed him.

"Wait," Patrick commanded and quickly unlocked a cabinet above the refrigerator. He pulled out a SIG Sauer P320 and a P226. He handed the second to Garrett along with a magazine.

"I'll call the police. Be careful," Imogen whispered before they went out the door.

As they ran down the street toward Harley's house, Patrick gave orders. "We'll approach the house from the lake side. He won't be able to see us coming from there. This way." Patrick cut down a driveway.

Garrett was glad that Patrick had his shit together, because he was struggling, but as they ran along the edge of the lake toward Harley's house, his training took over. He almost achieved the controlled but vigilant calm he experienced during missions. Almost. He'd never had so much at stake before.

For just a second, his mind went back to the mission in South America where Sebastian was killed. He'd been trying to get people to safety, despite the risk to himself. Garrett felt the guilt of his friend's death again, but he couldn't let that cloud what he was doing now. He'd failed Sebastian that day, but he wouldn't fail Harley.

He and Patrick approached the back of the house, each taking a corner and staying clear of windows. With the app, he unlocked the back door, grateful that Patrick had recommended that feature. Using the hand signals they used on missions, Patrick indicated that he'd work his way to the front of the house while Garrett slipped in the back.

Garrett paused for a second, listening, and heard voices in the living room. He caught the word "baby." Harley must have told Thomas about the child, hoping it would buy her some sympathy. Thomas was a selfish bastard, though, and Garrett doubted it would have any impact.

He flipped off the safety on the gun as he crossed soundlessly into the den. The pocket doors leading to the living room were partially open. That was good. He couldn't see Harley or Thomas yet, but their conversation was becoming more distinct.

"It's your child," Harley said. "Doesn't that mean anything to you?"

Garrett got closer to the door. Two more steps and he could be in the room with them.

"I think the baby goes first."

As Harley screamed, Garrett lunged inside, assessing the situation in a second. Thomas had her by the hair, knife poised to stab her in the stomach. Thankfully, the way the three of them were positioned gave Garrett a clear shot. Without hesitating, he squeezed off two rounds, hitting Thomas in the chest. The force of the impact knocked the man back and away from Harley. The knife skittered across the floor.

Patrick burst through the front door and charged into the room but lowered his weapon immediately when he saw that Thomas was down. In the distance, sirens wailed.

"I'll wait for the cops out front," Patrick said and disappeared.

"Is he… dead?" Harley's voice was barely audible.

"He's dead," Garrett confirmed. Thomas already had the stony features of a corpse. "Don't look, sweetheart." He placed the gun on an end table and pulled her into his arms, tucking her head against his shoulder. Shudders were going through her body, so he smoothed his hands down her back, hoping to offer some comfort.

It was over. As terrifying and horrible as it had been, it was finally, truly over.

16

———

Garrett closed the front door on the last of the police officers. Darkness had fallen outside as he'd answered the same questions multiple times, but he understood that a shooting fatality had to be properly investigated. He was glad they'd finished, though. It was only thanks to Patrick's and Kenton's pull in the community that it had gone as quickly as it had.

Maybe now he and Harley could talk.

She was seated at the dining room table with Violet, Mia, and Imogen. Her skin was pale, and he saw her hand shake as she lifted a glass of water to her lips. The four women were talking in low voices.

Everyone had shown up to support him and Harley. Patrick and Anderson had boarded up the smashed window, and Mia had gotten Harley to eat some soup she'd brought. That was one of the things he valued most about his group of friends: when things got tough, they were there without hesitation.

"I'm not going." Harley's voice rose. "I have to spend the night here.

I'm afraid if I leave, I won't come back. This is my house, and I'm staying."

The other women exchanged a glance. "I'll stay with you," Violet volunteered. "Anderson can take care of Nate for the night."

"I can stay." Garrett didn't want to be anywhere else. Harley had asked him to leave earlier, but things were different now, weren't they? Thomas was dead. The threat was gone.

"No," Harley said, looking straight at him. "Violet and I will be fine."

The determination in her expression hit him like a punch to the chest. He wanted to plead his case: being at her side was his responsibility. But maybe he'd forfeited that privilege. He had to respect her choice, as little as he liked it.

"If that's what you want," he said. "Thanks for coming, ladies." He nodded to the women and walked out onto the porch.

"Need a place for the night, Garrett? I need to get home, so our sitter can leave," Patrick said from where he stood in the shadows. Once the work inside was done, the other men had gone out to the porch to avoid crowding Harley.

"Guess so." It was surreal to think he was right back to where he'd been when he went to Patrick's earlier. Harley was safe now, though. If he couldn't be with her, at least he could take comfort in that.

"Come on over," Patrick said and then turned to the other SEALs. "You guys are welcome, too. I've got a good bottle of bourbon that I've been saving."

"Violet's mother is watching Nate, and I'll need to take over from her at some point, but I could come over for a bit," Anderson said.

"My mom has the girls, and I expect Mia will be heading home soon," Kenton said. "What about you, Matthew?"

"My time is my own." Like Garrett, Matthew didn't have the responsibility of a family. Garrett had always believed the two of them—and Sebastian—had the better approach to life, but now everything was different.

"See you all there, then," Patrick said.

Garrett went home with him and Imogen and walked out into the quiet backyard while they checked on their kids. Patrick had a good thing going here. A nice house and a loving family. Garrett had started imagining having those things with Harley.

Now that dream had slipped away, leaving him crushed—and it was his own fault. He'd screwed everything up between them.

"Light a fire, would you?" Patrick called from the back door. "Going to be chilly tonight."

Garrett wondered if Patrick realized he needed a task, something to keep his mind from going in circles. As he gathered wood from the pile alongside the garage and stacked it symmetrically in the fire ring, he thought about how the day's events had unfolded. He didn't for one second regret shooting Thomas. He only wished Harley hadn't gone through what she had or been witness to the killing.

As the fire started to crackle, his buddies came outside and gathered around. Patrick handed out glasses and poured bourbon for everyone. "This wasn't an official mission, but we can still toast its success. Harley's safe—and that asshole won't be hurting anyone else, either," he said. After they all took a drink, they settled into Adirondack chairs pulled up to the fire.

"Thomas is gone, and I'm glad about that, but I can't call the day a success," Garrett said.

"Give her time," Anderson advised. "She's dealing with a lot."

"So are you, Garrett," Kenton added. "Maybe it would help to talk it out. It's just us, and there's no judgment here."

Garrett looked to Matthew, who was holding the bourbon glass in his good hand, swirling the liquid absently. Matthew gave him a nod of encouragement. They were all friends, but Matthew knew him best and had probably already guessed what the heart of his problem was.

"I hate failing," Garrett said after a few minutes' silence. "And I've done it more lately than at any point in my life." No one commented, so he went on. "I failed Sebastian, and I failed Harley, too. Just in a different way."

"You saved Harley's life today," Patrick said. "And the baby's. That's a fact."

"After I put her in jeopardy." Harley had told him that serving Thomas with either the divorce papers or the restraining order would be like waving a red flag in front of a bull—but he hadn't listened. If that was why the man had chosen today to strike, the attack was Garrett's fault. In going behind Harley's back to try to protect her, he'd put her in more danger. Harley must have been terrified when she was alone with Thomas. She couldn't have known that he and Patrick were on the way. As it was, he'd gotten to her at the last possible moment. Five seconds more and Thomas would likely have stabbed her. Garrett would never be able to erase that scene from his mind—or forget how she shook in his arms afterward.

"That's not on you," Kenton said. "That was on her husband."

"But I promised her I'd keep her safe." He'd broken that promise, albeit unintentionally. "And Sebastian…" he started and then didn't know what to say next, so he drained his glass.

Matthew was studying him. "Is that where your head's going? To Colombia and the civilians that Sebastian was trying to get out? You didn't disappoint him, if that's what you're thinking."

Dammit. Matthew had nailed it. Garrett had had a flash of their last mission while running to Harley's house that afternoon. The situations seemed strangely similar. Sebastian had sacrificed himself trying to help others, but he'd only been in that position because of Garrett's choices. Then he'd entrusted his sister's safety to Garrett, and she'd ended up nearly stabbed by her abusive husband.

While the police were questioning him, he'd been able to keep those thoughts at bay, but they were back now. The two incidents were all mixed up in his mind.

"Why would you be responsible for what happened to Sebastian?" Kenton asked.

The three SEALs from the other team hadn't been there, so they didn't know all the details of the Colombian mission. They didn't know the guilt that Garrett carried with him.

"He isn't," Matthew said. "You tell it—or I will."

Garrett didn't want to. Sharing his emotions didn't come easily. But if he was going to, this was the right place. Reluctantly, Garrett explained how he and Sebastian had been up for too many hours and shouldn't have been on the raid.

"We operate like that all the time," Patrick said when Garrett paused. "We're experts on sleep deprivation in the field. What was different about this?"

"I was the one who insisted I was fine and wanted to go when the rest of the team moved on the compound. Since Sebastian and I did every-thing together, he volunteered, too. If he hadn't been on that raid, he'd still be alive. It's as simple as that. I made a choice that got my best friend killed."

"Bullshit," Anderson said. "You make him sound like he was a kid tagging along behind you. Sebastian was an adult and an experienced

SEAL. He made his own choice. I knew him well enough to be able to say that he wouldn't agree with your version of the story or with the fact that you're blaming yourself."

Garrett shook his head. Yeah, Anderson's reasoning was logical, but it didn't mitigate how he felt, and the situation with Harley compounded everything.

"I tried to tell you that weeks ago," Matthew said, "when you visited me in the hospital."

Matthew and the other injured SEALs had been medically evacuated ahead of the rest of the team. Once Garrett was stateside, he had gone directly to the hospital to visit Matthew. He remembered that conversation, but he'd been more concerned about Matthew than about delving into his own feelings. And that hadn't changed in the time since.

"Look," Kenton said. "The things we see as SEALs don't make for polite dinner conversation. It's some messy shit, and we each deal with it in our own way. As Mia likes to remind me, I make a plan and a contingency plan for everything, from a complex mission down to what to have for breakfast. It's my way of mentally managing things that are often uncontrollable in reality: I try to bring order to chaos. It doesn't always work, but it's how I handle what we do. We've all got something like that, but even with all those coping strategies, sometimes you've gotta just let those feelings boil over and come out. And that can take time. You need to give yourself that time."

"I'm not sure it will help. Nothing's going to change what happened." Garrett didn't want to let loose what he was feeling, because he feared it would overwhelm him.

"That's the point. What happened, happened. You've got to accept it," Anderson said.

"Your issue is that you think in extremes," Matthew said. "Either something was wholly successful, or it was a failure. There's not much room in between for you. Most of the time, you get to put stuff in the win column. You're lucky."

"So where the hell do I put Sebastian's death?" He couldn't just put it in the loss column and forget about it.

"That's a question you gotta answer for yourself. The mission happened, and there's nothing we can do to change how it played out. But it wasn't a total failure. Lots of civilians were saved, lots of drugs were kept out of circulation, and the aftermath led to you meeting and saving Harley. Despite the things that went wrong—and you know I'm not minimizing those—that part's a win. And I'm going to say it again: Sebastian made his own choices that day. Period."

It was weird to hear Matthew, who was usually ready to joke about anything, talk in such serious and gritty terms… but he was right. There had been good and bad results from the mission, and Garrett needed to accept both. Which meant trying to put aside his guilt over Sebastian.

That wasn't going to happen overnight. "Shit," Garrett said.

"Yeah," Matthew agreed. "Y'know, Sebastian would be pissed if he saw you beating yourself up like this. He'd tell you to go live your best life."

Garrett could hear Sebastian saying those words. He'd believed in helping his friends and enjoying every moment. If his life hadn't been cut short… But that was what Garrett was still wrestling with. "Not gonna be easy."

"Got that right," Matthew agreed. "Not easy for any of us. Our lives changed that day." Matthew had a physical reminder of that flawed mission, one that might prevent him from continuing in the career he loved. So much had been lost in that compound in Colombia, and none of them could explain exactly what had gone wrong.

"You need more time," Patrick said a minute later. "You should talk to your CO about staying stateside and doing the training gig for now."

He'd contacted his CO earlier in the evening to inform him of what had happened with Thomas. There would be more questions to answer as the Navy investigated the shooting, but Garrett wasn't worried about the outcome, since the security footage clearly showed he had discharged the weapon to defend Harley. Patrick's suggestion had merit, though. Garrett did need time to come to terms with Sebastian's death. He couldn't just stuff it down deep. He might wish he could, but that sort of thing would come back and bite him at the worst time. And falling apart at the worst time for a SEAL could mean more people would die.

And then there was Harley. Working at the base would keep him in the area, which might give him a chance with her. She was angry about what he'd done to push through the restraining order. He got that, and he understood her position. She'd had so little say in her own life, and her whole world was in turmoil. But now that he accepted that he'd been wrong, there was a chance that maybe, after a while, her irritation would fade.

Maybe they both needed time. And then… and then he'd see if they could find a way back to each other.

Because he wanted that. He hadn't realized how much until she'd sent him away.

17

Harley tucked some ginger chews into the outside pocket of the bag she'd packed for the day trip and walked down to the dock. Her boat bobbed on the water. She was going to have to make a decision about it once the probate was complete. Since she didn't know how to operate it, she should probably sell it, but she didn't think she could bring herself to do that. Like the house, it was part of Sebastian, and she wanted to cling to anything that had been his.

And that included his best friend. She sighed. She hadn't seen Garrett in a week. He was still in town, staying with Patrick and Imogen, but he hadn't approached her. He'd sent a few text messages asking if she was okay or needed anything, but that was all.

What they'd had for those brief weeks was over, which hurt, especially when she felt his presence all around her. He seemed to be everywhere she looked in her home, from the kitchen pantry to her now-lonely bed. Soon he'd be gone from the area, and that made her ache, too.

When a boat motored up to her dock and stopped, she pasted a smile on her face.

"Hi, girlfriend," Mia said. "Are you ready for our outing?" The SEAL wives had checked in on her daily, inviting her to come over for dinner or to go shopping. She'd declined most of the time, but the prospect of being outdoors on a beautiful spring day had been too appealing to turn down.

"As I'll ever be. I'm not sure about boats, but I'm willing to brave it." She was at the beginning of the second trimester. and her stomach was doing well in general. Still, she'd had a few bouts of morning sickness, and she didn't care to experience those again. How would her body react to riding in a boat? She was about to find out.

"Never been on one before?" Kenton asked as he offered his hand to help her board.

"Not even once. I know that's probably funny, coming from someone who lived in Florida, but it's true. I never had the opportunity." She stepped onto the boat. Mia and her nieces were sitting on cushions in the back, so she went to join them.

"I'll keep it steady for you," Kenton promised. "It's only about a twenty-minute ride out to the island." He and Matthew stood at the controls, and soon the boat was cutting through the water.

The lake was beautiful, blue and dazzling in the sunshine. A breeze ruffled her hair, and she felt okay for the first few minutes. Then a wave smacked the boat, rolling it from side to side. Harley gulped in some air as she felt her stomach churn.

"Okay?" Mia asked, touching her arm lightly.

"Yeah. I think so." She reached for one of the ginger chews that Garrett had bought her and popped it into her mouth. Other times when she'd been queasy, they'd helped. Unfortunately, they also made her think of Garrett and how caring he'd been. She wanted to sigh again, but she didn't let herself.

"I'm glad you're coming with us today," Mia said, seeming to sense her shift in mood.

"I couldn't say no. Today is too nice, and I had to get out of the house."

"It's a big place to live in by yourself."

"There's that." Harley felt brave for going on a boat ride, but the true test of bravery would be moving on after the deaths of her brother and husband. She didn't grieve for Thomas, but it was still a traumatic event.

And then there was the loss of Garrett from her life. Somehow, even though he was still alive and well, his absence was more poignant than Sebastian's.

"Is it Garrett?" Mia asked quietly, so Kenton and Matthew couldn't hear her.

Harley winced. She didn't really want to talk about it, but Mia was so kind that she found herself doing just that. "Yes. I... I don't know how to think about what we had. Was it a true relationship? Or just a fling because of our shared grief over Sebastian and the fact that we happened to be living in the same house?"

"But you miss him?"

"Yeah, I do." So damn much. The boat swayed just then, and a little spray came up over the side, misting over them.

"Sorry," Kenton said, turning from the controls to address them. "The wind's shifting, but I'll get us to smoother waters."

"No worries," Mia called.

"You're lucky. He's a good one," Harley said with a nod toward Kenton.

"They all are, including Garrett." Mia gazed at her husband, love clear in her expression, then turned back to face Harley. "I'm just going to say this: SEALs can be tough to love at first, because they don't do anything by half measures. If there's a problem, they pursue a solution relentlessly. If they need to protect, they do it with everything they've got. But they love that way, too." Mia smiled. "I have to remind myself of that sometimes, when I get irritated with Kenton for being over the top."

Harley saw the truth in that. Garrett was definitely the all-in type, and that had its benefits. The vast number of projects he'd completed on the house in a few short weeks proved that. But that trait had also led him to take away something precious to her: her control. She didn't know if that need to take the reins without consulting her was something Garrett would be willing to change—and if not, whether she could live with that the way Mia had learned to. She still yearned for him, though.

She sat back against the cushion and tried to enjoy the ride as Mia pointed out birds and cloud shapes for her nieces. The water didn't get any rougher, but Harley's tolerance for it waned. She was grateful to reach the small island, where she saw another boat was already docked. She'd thought it was just going to be their group.

"How'd you like the ride?" Kenton asked as he helped her off the boat.

"I'll leave being in the Navy to you. I think I'm a landlubber." She kept her tone playful, but she was thrilled to be on stable ground. "Being on boats is definitely not for me." She turned when she heard laughter behind her—a deep chuckle that she recognized.

Garrett was standing farther down the dock with Patrick, Imogen, and their kids. His white-blond hair shone in the sunshine as he met her gaze. He looked so good she wanted to run to him and wrap her arms around him. But she couldn't do that. And she couldn't leave, either. Somehow, she was going to have to spend the day with him.

The worst of it would be managing her emotions with so many eyes on her. She felt the weight of the others' expectations. They were all hoping for a happily ever after for her and Garrett.

"Ahoy," Violet called as a third boat nosed into the dock with Anderson at the wheel, holding their son, Nate, in one arm. "I guess we're the last ones to the party."

Harley moved to greet them, glad both to have attention shift away from her and to see Violet, who stepped on to the dock and pulled her into a hug. "It'll be okay," Violet whispered. "We're all friends here. Just enjoy yourself."

"I'll try." She forced a smile. She'd do her best to have fun. And it was a big enough group that she wouldn't be alone with Garrett. She didn't even have to talk to him directly if she didn't want to.

Did she want to?

The answer to that question was irrelevant. What they had was over. They just happened to be at the same party. No big deal.

To avoid her uncomfortable feelings, Harley turned her attention to helping unload the boats. No one would let her pick up the heavier coolers, but there was still plenty for her to do as they transported the picnic supplies to a small beach area.

The guys set up a volleyball net while Harley and the other women spread out picnic blankets and unpacked food. But then, as Harley was opening one of the coolers, Garrett came toward her, reaching for a beer. Without thinking, she scrambled away.

Her escape was blocked by the water behind her, and she almost panicked. Then she saw Ava and Emma on the beach, so she seized the opportunity to go play with them.

"What should we draw?" she asked the girls, trying to sound casual. They each had a plastic trowel and were carving patterns in the sand.

"A flower," Ava said.

"No, a heart," Emma replied.

"Flower." Ava's chin jutted out.

"Heart." Emma's hands went to her hips.

Uh-oh. Harley might have gone from the frying pan into the fire. She had no idea how to defuse the disagreement between the girls, but she couldn't walk away, either, because six feet three inches of Navy SEAL was between her and the other adults.

"Ask Harley to draw you a heart with a flower in it," Mia called from where she was preparing sandwiches.

Bless her, Harley thought.

"Can you?" the girls said in unison.

"I think so." Harley dropped to her knees and carefully drew the outline of a heart. "Good?"

"Now, a flower. Right there." Ava pointed to the center of the heart.

Harley wasn't a great artist, but she did her best to draw a flower that looked like a daisy. When she looked up for the girls' approval, Garrett still stood only feet away, staring at her. She dropped her head, letting her hair hide her face.

"Garrett, can you move this for me?" That was Imogen's voice, and Harley said another word of thanks for kind friends. Sure, they'd tried to toss her and Garrett together, but they'd also picked up on how uncomfortable she was.

"Time to eat," Violet announced a moment later, and Harley let herself be drawn along with Ava and Emma to a blanket where Ellery appeared to be in charge. The grade-school-age girl carefully arranged their plates, cups, and napkins. She was doing exactly what Harley had always wanted to do as a child, except the food at this little party was real.

Her mind flashed back to when Garrett played along with her imaginary tea party in the secret room and then leaned over the table for their first kiss. Involuntarily, her eyes went to him. He was sitting on a log next to Matthew, smiling at something his friend said. He seemed to feel her attention, though, because he looked over and caught her staring at him. Their gazes held, the seconds ticking away, as longing filled her. She didn't know what to do. Fortunately, before she had to decide, one of the girls asked her a question and brought her focus back to safer subjects.

Throughout the afternoon, she kept busy playing with the kids or talking with everyone but Garrett. As the hour grew later, she grew more confident that she could get through this.

"Last game: everybody plays," Anderson announced. Various groups had played volleyball over the course of the day, but Harley had only played once—during the time when Garrett had gone on a nature walk with the kids.

"I can spike." Matthew held up his good hand with a lopsided smile.

"Take your position near the net," Anderson said and directed the others onto teams. "Okay, Mia and Harley, you're with Garrett and Matthew. That puts Imogen, Violet, Patrick, and me on a team."

"I don't need to play," Harley said. "I can watch the kids."

Anderson pointed to a blanket under a shade tree where the younger kids were sound asleep and Ellery was reading a book. She looked up with a wave and a smile. "We've got that covered."

With no graceful way to get out of it, Harley took her place near the net, conscious of the fact that Garrett was directly behind her. He served, and the volley began. The action went quickly, forcing Harley to stay on her toes. She managed to bump and spike without getting too near Garrett.

"Match point," Anderson yelled a little while later, as he served for his team. The ball was headed in her direction but slightly over her head. She could leap for it. As she started to, she realized that Garrett was going for it, too, and she pulled back to avoid contact with him.

"Got it," he said and spiked the ball. His angle was off, sending the ball out of bounds and giving the other team their final point.

"That's what I'm talking about!" Anderson and Patrick did a victory dance on their side of the net.

"Sorry," Harley murmured, knowing that she could have prevented the win if she hadn't been so jumpy around Garrett.

"Listen up," Kenton called. "We need to pack up and be on the boats at eighteen hundred hours so we're off the water and home before dark. That's twenty minutes from now. Here are your assignments." He gave orders to everyone. When he got to Garrett and Harley, he said, "You two are in charge of outdoor equipment. That gets stowed on Anderson's boat."

"I'll gather up the balls and sand toys," she volunteered.

"Mia's got that as part of kid duty." Garrett pointed to where Mia was having the kids put their play items in a basket. "Help me take the volleyball net down?"

Since she didn't see an alternative, she worked with him in silence for the first few minutes, but that seemed even more awkward than stilted conversation would be. "When do you deploy?" she finally asked. She had the irrational hope that things would be easier for her once he was gone. At the same time, she dreaded that he'd be far away and in danger. It was an emotional seesaw that she didn't know how to balance.

"I'm not deploying," he said. "I've requested the training position stateside."

"And that was granted?" She'd always been under the impression that he'd have to go wherever the Navy decided to send him.

"Under the circumstances, yes."

"What circumstances?" Did he mean because his previous mission was still being investigated, or was it something else?

"Harley—" Garrett started.

"Ticktock, people. Let's get loaded," Kenton yelled.

Harley glanced at Kenton in time to see Mia put her hand on his arm as if to cut him off, but it was too late. Garrett was already turning away, shouldering the bag that contained the net. Whatever he had been going to say was lost.

18

Harley connected her Bluetooth speaker to her phone and blasted her favorite tunes as she cleaned up the kitchen. The music banished the house's silence, but it did nothing to fill the space. She did a little twirl after putting the freshly washed dishes away, trying to pump herself up. But it was pointless.

She was lonely, and she didn't like it. It made no sense. She'd lacked meaningful connections to others for most of her life—and she had them now. Mia, Violet, and Imogen had taken turns staying with her for several days after the attack, and she could call any of them up to talk… but it wasn't enough. Not anymore.

The song shifted to something slower and romantic. It was a piece she'd loved when she was younger and full of hope that she'd find forever love. Thomas had taught her a hard lesson about that, but then Garrett had come into her life. And for a while, everything had changed.

He'd filled her home with his strong, loving presence, and she'd come to rely on him. She'd dreamed of a future with him, and it had seemed within her grasp right up until he'd let her down and she'd sent him away. He'd still swooped in to save her from Thomas, but she felt cut off from him now. Adrift.

Seeing him at the island had only reinforced how much she missed him. And what had her reaction been? To avoid him, which was stupid. She should have taken the opportunity to talk with him and to judge if he felt for her what she did for him.

She'd come home that night and been unable to sleep. She'd wandered the house in the quiet darkness, wrestling with her own feelings and wondering what he had been about to say to her as they were packing up. Before the sun rose, she'd arrived at a truth: she was in love with Garrett, but she wasn't sure how to reach out to him.

And she was chicken. She'd been rejected so many times in her life, and she feared she wouldn't be able to take it if she poured out her heart only to learn that Garrett didn't share her feelings. So she'd done nothing except let more time pass. She tossed the kitchen towel down in annoyance. She needed to see him. Now. It couldn't wait any longer.

If he said there was no room for her in his life, she'd find a way to accept that. But at least she would know.

She shut off the music and went to dial his number. But in the sudden silence, she heard the pounding of a hammer outside. The contractor she'd hired to finish up a few projects wasn't there that day, so the sound surprised her.

With a sudden swelling of hope, she rushed to the front door. She disengaged the alarm and stepped onto the porch.

There he was, assembling a large wooden box. She felt her heart thud in her chest. In the bed of his truck, she saw bags of topsoil and flats of little plants. She took all that in in one sweep before returning her attention to Garrett.

"Garrett." She couldn't get out more than that. He'd come to her, and she needed to know why.

"Hi, Harley." He put his hammer down. Usually, he had an easy smile, but that was gone. His expression was… uncertain. "I'm… I'm making your garden."

"My garden?"

"Yeah. You said you wanted to grow vegetables, and I talked you out of it." She remembered that conversation at the nursery. "I was wrong about that. You have plenty of sunshine if you choose the right spots in your yard, and I'm building you raised beds, so you won't have to bend over so far to tend your plants."

"That's sweet of you," she said. "It means a lot to me."

He took a few steps toward the porch. "I was wrong about other things, too. I should have listened to what *you* wanted and not been so focused on doing what I thought was right."

"That's who you are." She'd come to understand that, with some help from her friends. SEALs were SEALs. They were wired a certain way, but that didn't mean they couldn't learn to compromise. Was this his gesture to show he could? Oh, how she hoped it was.

"It shouldn't be," he said. "Not when it comes to you. Harley, I'm so sorry. I got so caught up in fixing the house and keeping my word to Sebastian and then dealing with the threat from Thomas that I didn't even realize I was falling in love with you. I *am* in love with you."

"You are?" Her voice was a whisper. All those years of being alone and isolated melted away at his words.

"Completely. But I get it if I have to earn your trust again. I'll do whatever it takes to get back to where we were." He drew even nearer, until he was on the bottom step looking up at her. "I don't want to control you. I want to love you. I want to live in this house with you. I want to live my life with you so we can share everything. The good, the bad, and all of it in between. If you'll give me the chance."

His expression was so earnest that she started to smile, and that seemed to give him the ability to go on making his case. "I want to be with you when this garden produces tomatoes and cucumbers. I want to build a swing set in the yard. I want to be here when the baby's born, and I want to give him or her brothers and sisters."

The baby she was carrying wasn't Garrett's, but she felt confident there would be no difference to him between this child and those the two of them might have together.

"I want all that, but I also know it's not easy being with a SEAL." Doubt crept back into his expression. "I'll be deployed for stretches, but I'll always come home to you as soon as I can. I promise you that."

She went down two steps, so she was perched on the one just above where he stood, putting them at eye level. She rested her hands lightly on his shoulders. "Are you done?"

"I could say more, but it all boils down to: I love you and want to be with you," he said, eyes burning with hope.

"Okay, I've got a few things to say now," she said. "I want you to know that being with you has opened up my world. For the first time ever, I'm connected to people and a place. I can't even express how magical that is to me. I belong here. I feel that. And as wonderful as that is, knowing I have your love makes it better."

"You do have it." He smiled for the first time since they'd started talking, and his hands came to rest on her waist. "All of it. All of me."

"Good. Because I need you so that this beautiful house can become a home. Our home. I love you, Garrett. Without you, this is just a pretty place. But with you, we can make the life I've always dreamed of. I know it's not going to be perfect, and when you're deployed, I'll miss you like crazy. But I'll have friends to help get me through. When you come back to me, those are going to be incredibly special days."

"And nights?" he asked, pulling her against him.

"Definitely, the nights." She stroked her fingers over his cheekbones, drawing out the moment. She intended to kiss him until their lips went numb, but first she wanted to preserve this memory. She liked that it took place on the steps of the porch she already loved. This exact spot was going to be the scene of many happy reunions for years to come.

He took one of her hands and kissed her palm before his lips moved to the inside of her wrist and began a slow, torturous trip to her mouth. When he finally reached it and kissed her fully, it was worth the wait. After a few more minutes, he scooped her up and headed for the front door.

"What about the garden?" she asked, resting her head on his shoulder.

"Later," he said. "For now, I want to love every part of you."

Nothing had ever sounded better. Once they were inside, he closed the front door behind them, and together they opened the way to their future.

END OF THE SEAL'S PREGNANT ROOMMATE
HARTSVILLE'S SEAL HEROES BOOK FOUR

The SEAL's Convenient Wife, 31 December 2020

The SEAL's Surprise Baby, 7 January 2021

The SEAL's Instant Family, 14 January 2021

The SEAL's Pregnant Roommate, 23 February 2022

The SEAL's Treatment, 2 March 2023

The SEAL's Hookup, 9 March 2023

PS: Do you like sexy military men? Turn the page for an exclusive free book offer and exclusive extracts from **The SEAL's Treatment, The SEAL's Virgin Lover** and **Gage.**

FREE BOOK OFFER

Read FIVE full-length romances by USA Today best-selling author Leslie North for FREE! Over 600+ pages of best-selling romance with hundreds of FIVE STAR REVIEWS!

<u>Sign-up to her mailing list and get your FREE books</u>

THANK YOU!

Thank you so much for purchasing my book. It's hard for me to put into words how much I appreciate my readers. If you enjoyed this book, please remember to leave a review. Reviews are crucial for an author's success and I would greatly appreciate it if you took the time to review the book. I love hearing from you!

You can connect with me on:

MAKE AN AUTHOR'S DAY

There's nothing better than reading great reviews from readers like yourself, but there's more to it than simply putting a smile on my face. As an independent author, I don't have the financial might of a big NYC publishing house or the clout to get in Oprah's book club. What I do have, as my not-so-secret weapon is you, my awesome readers!

If you enjoyed this book, I'd be incredibly grateful if you could leave a quick review. No matter the length (short is fine!), your review will help this series get the exposure it needs to grow and make it into the hands of other awesome readers. Plus, reading your kind reviews is often the highlight of my day, so please be sure to let me know what you loved most about this book.

ABOUT LESLIE

Leslie North is the USA Today Bestselling pen name for a critically-acclaimed author of women's contemporary romance and fiction. The anonymity gives her the perfect opportunity to paint with her full artistic palette, especially in the romance and erotic fantasy genres.

To find your next Leslie North book visit LeslieNorthBooks.com or choose:

BY TROPE

BY HERO

PS: Want sneak peeks, giveaways, ARC offers, fun extras and plenty of pictures of bad boys? Join my Facebook group, Leslie's Lovelies!

BLURB

She's helping heal his body, but what about his heart?

Physical therapist Kinley James loves helping her clients—until she accidentally discovers one of them is a Mafia hit man. Now she's seen too much, and that means her life is in danger. Good thing her sexy new client, Matthew Templeton, is a rugged Navy SEAL.

Matthew is struggling to recover from a serious injury and learn how to be a dad to his recently orphaned niece. He's committed to powering through his rehab so he can return to the job he loves—and he's less than delighted when Kinley warns that may not be realistic. Still, not only is she a warm and beautiful woman, she's amazing with his niece.

And there's not a chance in hell that he'll let any harm come to her.

At first, Kinley dismisses the increasingly dangerous "accidents" happening around her, but Matthew is worried… and neither can dismiss their growing attraction to each other. Can Matthew protect Kinley, and confess his feelings for her, before it's too late?

Grab your copy of *The SEAL's Treatment*
www.LeslieNorthBooks.com

~

EXCERPT

Chapter one

Matthew Templeton unstrapped his niece from the car seat, balanced her on one hip, and shouldered her Disney Princess backpack. The child-sized bag just fit over his arm. Since his still-healing right hand wouldn't grip the thin straps, it was the best way for him to carry it.

As they walked up the front steps to Kenton and Mia's Victorian-style home, Anaya turned her face into Matthew's neck. "Scared," she whispered.

"Nothing to be scared of, sweetie. These are my friends." And frankly, they were a godsend, stepping in to babysit for him like this —not that he expected a two-year-old to understand that. No, all

Anaya knew was that Mommy was gone and everything was new and strange now.

He hated having to leave her in an unfamiliar house with people she didn't know, after all that had happened. Anaya seemed to have accepted that her mama wasn't coming home, but that experience had, understandably, left her uncertain and insecure at times. Matthew himself was still coming to grips with it—his older sister's death in a car crash three weeks earlier had walloped him, especially since it meant that the two-year-old in his arms had no one left in the world but him.

Growing up, it had only ever been him, his mom, and his sister. Mom had passed three years ago. And now Candace was gone, and she'd named Matthew as Anaya's guardian. The courts would make it all official once Candace's will was through probate. The reality was already here: Matthew now had a child.

Not something he'd ever expected. He'd make it work, though. Somehow.

The decorative wooden door opened before Matthew had a chance to knock. "Hey, there," Kenton said. Behind him, his twin toddlers, Emma and Ava, dashed forward to see who their visitors were.

"Is it the girl to play with us?" Ava asked.

Anaya lifted her head, and the glimmer of a smile showed on her face when she saw the twins.

"This is Anaya," Matthew said.

"Come on." Emma gestured. "We're playing dress-up."

"Okay?" Matthew asked his niece, who was already squirming to get down. A second later, the girls ran into the living room. That was a relief. "I really appreciate this," he told Kenton. "I've got to get this physical therapy started."

"No worries. I'm a pro at managing little girls. I've read all the books." Kenton chuckled when Matthew shot him a skeptical look. "Okay, so I *did* read the books, but most of what I know comes from practical experience. She'll be fine."

"I figured as much, but it's the first time I've left her since I went to Charleston to get her." Matthew knew he had to get going. Still, it was tough leaving Anaya behind, even with a fellow SEAL who Matthew would trust with his own life.

"Go, take a couple hours for yourself, and see what Dr. James can do for your hand. She's the best."

"I know, I know. It's why I'm here." Matthew had temporarily relocated to Hartsville to work with the well-regarded hand specialist, but living near a number of SEAL buddies was good, too, especially after their last mission went sideways, causing the injury that sent everything spiraling off course.

He had to concentrate on healing, so he could return to active duty. His hand was better after the surgeries, but it was a long way from 100 percent. Every day he struggled to complete basic tasks, and now with Anaya to care for… Life had thrown him some hella big curveballs in the past few months.

But he *would* get things back on track. He'd see what Dr. James prescribed for therapy and give it his all. He'd have a purpose then, which would be way better than the waiting around he'd done post-op and while the burns healed.

"Daddy, will you be the prince?" Emma ran to Kenton and grabbed his hand. The other girls followed. Anaya already had a crown on her head and a string of beads around her neck. She *was* fine, which meant Matthew could go.

"Give me a hug." He knelt down and opened his arms to her. She gave him a swift, tight hug before running off with the other girls.

"See you later—and take your time," Kenton called as he followed the kids into the living room. "I've got this."

Matthew let himself out and drove to the medical center. He checked in at the physical therapist's office and took a seat, keeping his eye on his phone to see if Kenton texted. He knew he needed to stop worrying. Anaya would be okay without him. He wasn't so sure how he felt being without her, though. A little lost, maybe.

The three weeks since Candace's death had passed in a blur. Two weeks spent in Charleston and then back to Hartsville to rent a house and learn how to care for a toddler. His buddies had all called with offers to help, but he'd wanted to keep it just him and Anaya at first. The social worker who interviewed him as part of the guardianship process had said that they needed to create a bond.

He thought they'd done that, and it had given him purpose and focus to care for her, even if he struggled with the physical aspects.

"Matthew?" a petite woman in black athletic pants and a bright blue shirt called as she came through a door.

"That's me." He stood and strode toward her, automatically sticking out his right hand to shake hers. It was a habit that he couldn't break, even when his hand had still been bandaged.

"Nice to meet you. I'm Dr. James—or Kinley, if you prefer." She gave his hand a light squeeze, gentle enough not to hurt. He liked that she didn't hesitate, that she didn't treat him like he had to be handled with kid gloves. Her eyes left his face to track down his arm to where their palms met. Was she assessing him already?

"Follow me." She led him past a small gym area to a medical consultation room. "We'll be in here today for the assessment." She turned and watched him enter the space, her head tilted slightly to the side. "Go ahead and have a seat on the table."

He hated the padded tables with their crinkly paper, as well as the questions that he knew would be coming, but at least she was more pleasant than some of the military doctors he'd seen. He studied her as she flipped open a laptop. Her brown hair, pulled into a ponytail, looked soft and wavy. He found himself wondering what it would look like down. She had big, brown eyes that seemed to draw him in. And, while he was well aware she was his physical therapist, not a potential date, it was impossible for him not to notice how her fit, but curvy body moved as she walked.

Whatever he'd imagined Dr. James would look like wasn't this, and she was years younger than he'd expected her to be, given the reputation she'd built in her field. About his age, if he had to guess.

She sat on a low swivel stool and turned her attention to him, her expression professional but warm. "I've read the reports from your surgeries and the notes from the Navy physicians, but I like to get a sense of the situation directly from the patient. I understand that it's not a lot of fun to talk about, and that you've probably gone over it a million times already, but it'll really help me help you if you tell me how the injury occurred."

He raised an eyebrow. SEAL missions were classified, and this one was still under investigation by the brass because it had gone so wrong. His team member and friend, Sebastian Valenti, had made the ultimate sacrifice at that drug-processing compound in Colombia. And Matthew wasn't the only one who'd ended up in the hospital.

"Just how you were injured," she said when he hesitated. "I don't need to know any specifics you can't tell me. This is about you, not about the mission. You already did your job there—now it's my turn to do mine, here."

Strangely enough, thinking of it that way helped. "All right." He ran his left hand over his face, trying to decide where to start the narrative. "I was... I was attempting to defuse a bomb that was ticking down. It was a complex mechanism, designed to… that doesn't matter. I had my right glove off for better dexterity. In the end, I stayed with it a little longer than I should have."

"So the force of the blast broke the bones and caused the burns?"

"Yeah, but I was also thrown backward and landed on my right hand." The pain had been so intense, he'd feared his hand had been blown off. He'd been damn lucky that it hadn't been—and that he hadn't sustained any other significant injury.

"That's consistent with what the initial X-rays showed," she commented. "All right. Can you tell me what outcome you're looking for from this therapy?"

Wasn't it obvious? "I need to get back to active duty."

"As a demolitions expert?"

"Well, yeah."

"Any other goals?"

"I recently took guardianship of my niece. Her mother, my sister, was killed in a car accident. Anaya's only two, so I need to be able to care for her. The hand"—he raised it—"makes helping her dress and tying her shoes tough." Among other things. Doing Anaya's hair was nearly impossible, but that was partly due to his lack of skill and experience.

"A two-year-old?" Her voice softened. "The poor child, to lose her mother like that. And you, too—your sister. I'm sorry."

He nodded. He was never sure what to say when people offered him sympathy. His go-to when he was uncomfortable was to crack a joke. Not in this situation, though. There wasn't any humor in it.

"Looking after a child is definitely challenging, but I think it's wonderful that you're stepping up to take care of her. I'll do whatever I can to help you get back the dexterity you'll need. For now, let's get started with the physical exam." Her tone was matter-of-fact as she explained what she'd need from him. "Lie on your back for this first part. You're going to feel some discomfort, but if there's actual pain, you need to tell me."

Matthew lay on his back with his right side nearer to her as she examined his shoulder and elbow, bending his arm in various ways. After several minutes, she had him sit up so she could take his wrist and turn it, flipping his hand over and back. When his breath hitched slightly, she paused. "Pain?"

"It's fine," he said. "Don't worry about it, Dr. James."

She shook her head, firmly holding eye contact in a way that said she meant business. "It's my job to worry about it. I'm going to work with the hand directly next. I need you to be honest with me about the pain level." Her slim fingers felt around his wrist and palm. When she pressed into the base of his palm, a streak of pain shot up his arm— and from the look in her eyes, she could tell. He wasn't used to women he'd just met being able to read him that well, but he got the sense that those warm brown eyes never missed a thing. They were assessing, but, as the pain lessened, all he could see was how beautiful they were. He put the inappropriate thought aside.

"Squeeze my fingers." She held out two of hers. He took them in his and squeezed lightly. "Go ahead. You won't hurt me." He tightened his grip, but he could feel that it wasn't what it had once been.

"I lost some strength when my hand was bandaged up after the surgeries." He didn't like appearing weak in front of her, but he'd recover what he'd lost. He had to: his future depended on it. The Navy was the only life he knew—the only one that had been good for him, at least. He needed the discipline imposed by the military.

Grab your copy of *The SEAL's Treatment*
www.LeslieNorthBooks.com

BLURB

Danger and desire are an intoxicating mix…

Navy SEAL Gage Jackelson will do anything to solve the murder of his friend… even get half-naked for a romance-novel cover shoot. It doesn't hurt that the photographer is equally gorgeous and intriguing. But Anna Middleton is a distraction he can't afford. Could she know more than she's letting on? He'll have to get close to her to find out. Really close.

Ever since Gage showed up, Anna's quiet life has been turned upside down. First, her billionaire boss disappeared after an explosion rocked their office building. Then some decidedly sinister characters started following her. And the smoking-hot SEAL is driving her wild—not that she's complaining.

She meant to keep their relationship strictly professional. But as they become further entangled in a web of danger, Anna can't help falling hard. They'll need to work together to make it through…but will Gage stick around once he's ensured Anna's safety?

Grab your copy of *Gage (SEAL Team Ten Book One)* from www.LeslieNorthBooks.com

~

EXCERPT

Chapter one

Gage Jackelson decided he'd rather be in the middle of a firefight on open water than standing in front of a green screen in nothing more than his jeans, feeling like a hunk of meat on a slab.

A Goth pixie—heavy on the black eyeliner and dyed hair and complete with a pink tutu trimmed in more black—flitted about him, dusting powder on him and muttering about cheekbones.

This was ridiculous. He stood, arms folded, wondering how he could get out of this. But he couldn't. He had to start thinking of this like a mission. So he let the pixie fuss.

The elevator pinged, and he hoped the photographer had finally arrived so he could wrap up this charade, get the intel they needed, and get his shirt back on. The things he'd do for a friend—even a dead one.

He glanced over and watched a young woman walk into the studio—okay, warehouse was a better name for it. A loft, big and drafty and empty except for all the photography equipment. Concrete floors, high ceilings, stark white walls. Dirt glazed the windows, but there were enough lights on him that he kept breaking a light sweat.

The woman approached, head cocked, and stared at him. He could feel his skin warm under her scrutiny, which was just another sign of how screwed up this situation was. Normally he *liked* it when women checked him out. He and the US Navy had worked damn hard to give him this body, and he was proud of it. But normally he wasn't on display like he was something for sale.

Eyes blue as the Mediterranean Sea fixed on him. Tight jeans encased long legs—he'd always been a leg man—and a white silk blouse said she had enough money to afford good clothes. Golden hair had been pulled back from a heart-shaped face. She didn't wear much makeup that he could see, and he caught a flash of gold earrings. But those eyes kept pulling him back for another look. Who the hell was she? The photographer's girlfriend?

No, he realized in the next instant, and he kicked himself for making foolish assumptions as the woman turned and walked over to the camera—not a digital model, but something big and old and expensive-looking. She stared through the lens and then looked up at him. "Gage Jackelson." She said the name as if she was thinking of something else. She propped a fist on one hip. "I keep wondering why a Navy SEAL would agree to do a cover shoot." A guy could feel quite warm wrapped up in her sultry tone.

He lifted an eyebrow. He had reasons, all right. But they were his business, not hers. "And you are?" he asked instead.

She stepped up and reached out to shake his hand. "Anna Middleton."

Gage nodded. He fought the urge to hold her hand longer than he should. She tilted her head up to look at him, and he could swear he caught a hint of surprise in those sea-blue eyes.

She pulled her hand back, and he watched as she tucked it behind her back before grabbing the camera off its stand. "Did Linda explain how this works?"

Linda—the pixie—flashed a smile at him. She trailed a finger down his forearm. "You'll do great. He's set, Anna." She ducked away.

Gage turned his focus back to Anna. "How hard is it to smile for the camera?" Gage drawled. His fingers hadn't stopped tingling since he touched her, and he was itching to do so again.

"You'd be surprised." The corners of her wide mouth twitched. "We'll start without props, but Linda will bring a few in later."

"Props?" Gage lifted both eyebrows.

Anna took a couple of shots, the camera clicking. "We use a green screen so we can drop in any background, but it's easier to use physical objects for anything that you will be touching in the actual photos." Stepping back to the tripod, Anna set the camera on it. She looked through the camera lens, paused, and looked back up at him. "Um, you're looking a little stiff."

Linda gave a snort of amusement, though she was polite enough to try to hide it with a cough. Gage smiled, and Anna gave Linda a dirty look before turning back to Gage. "Any chance you can relax? Loosen up? Look less like you're standing in front of a camera?"

Gage forced a smile. He was going to kill Scotty and Spencer for talking him into being the one to come and gather intel from Coran Williams Publishing. *This is for Nick*, he told himself again. Their brother in arms had been killed, shot down in circumstances that were sketchy as hell. With every mission, there was always the chance that someone wouldn't come back, but this mess stank to high heaven and had left them all with an endless list of questions and absolutely no answers.

No answers *yet*. The team wouldn't stop searching until they found out what was going on, even if they had damn little to go on right now —just an encrypted flash drive and one personal photo of Nick and his wife, Natalie. They hadn't even found Nick's awards and honors for service. But the photo had led them here.

"Mr. Jackelson?"

Gage shook himself out of his mood—he'd been starting to frown. He had to watch that. They'd all talked it over and agreed that busting in here with questions wouldn't get them far. They needed everyone's guards down, needed to get natural, honest answers to their questions —and they needed to get inside this place and poke around. Which was why he was here. With his shirt off.

"It's Lieutenant." The correction was automatic but quiet. Not like he was in uniform so she'd know. "Lieutenant Jackelson, or Gage."

She nodded, but the smile looked forced now. "Lieutenant, it would be nice if you seemed a bit less—"

"Stiff?" Gage offered a smile.

"Uncomfortable. Why don't you tell us a story or describe something in detail?"

"Like a first date?" She huffed, and he had to admit that he was enjoying flustering her.

That wide mouth of hers tightened. "How about instructions for changing a tire? Or you could talk about SEAL training. The point is to stop thinking about what you're doing."

And how my shirt's missing. Gage realized she was right. He needed to get out of his head. He needed to stop thinking about why he was really there. He wasn't going to be able to search the place any time soon—not with all the people scurrying around to help with the shoot—but he had a great view to check security and access for later.

He already knew Nick's wife Natalie was linked to this organization. He just needed to figure out how. And if he could uncover any hints as to where the hell she was, that would be great, too.

Natalie hadn't shown up for Nick's funeral or his wake. They were still trying to track her down in the hopes that she might know something about why Nick had been killed. A photo on the cover of a book had led them here—and Gage drew the short straw for the initial recon.

When he'd walked in the door, the receptionist—or whoever the person was who was checking people in—had assumed he was there for the casting call to hire a cover model. That was too good an opportunity to turn down…and the fact that he'd beaten out all the pros and gotten hired on the spot had been a nice ego boost. He'd played it that he could use the extra cash, but now that he was stuck here, he was starting to wonder if he should have just broken in after hours.

"Lieutenant?" That husky, sexy voice snapped him out of his thoughts again. He looked at Anna and found her blue eyes starting to sizzle with irritation. "If this is too much for you—"

Holding up his hand, Gage stopped her. "I got it. A story." He stared at her.

Eyebrows lifting, she asked, "What's it like being a SEAL?"

He shrugged. "I wouldn't know what it's like not being one."

"You started young."

He shrugged. "We all start young—it's not a game for old guys."

"A game?"

"When you're out on a mission, you tend to look at it as something to be conquered. It's win or lose, and losing is not an option. It's also fun. You jump out of airplanes and helicopters, swim in some of the worst ocean currents. You're freezing, you're sweating, and you hike some incredibly dangerous terrain."

"That's what you consider fun?" She sounded skeptical.

He flashed her a sly smile. "I think *lots* of things are fun. Basically, anything that gets your heart racing."

She flushed a little at that. "And when you have time off?"

His smile slipped into a smirk. "Some of us have been known to go looking for trouble. Or trouble finds us."

"Which brings you here." She started snapping photos. "Keep going. You do this alone?"

"Hell, no. You're a team. *We're* a team."

She looked up from her camera and asked, "And what are they like, your team? Go ahead and move as you talk. You don't have to stand still."

He nodded. And stayed where he was, arms crossed. "Well…my team leader fancies himself a bit of a ladies' man. He's got more exes spread across this beautiful country than I have teeth, but he's damn good at his job. Then there's our sniper."

"Yeah? What's he like?" she prompted.

"He's…well, he's the typical redhead. A hothead, except in action he is one cool dude."

Anna grabbed the camera and circled around him. "Linda, bring in a hat."

Gage lifted his eyebrows. A hat? Linda grinned at him and put a straw Stetson on his head. She gave him a wink.

From behind her camera, Anna asked in that low voice of hers, "What about you, Lieutenant? What's your role on the team?"

Gage pulled the Stetson down to a better angle. "I'm the demolitions guy. My expertise is things that go boom." He liked the science of it —understanding all the components, figuring out the factors he'd need to control to get exactly the outcome he wanted. Plus, it was just fun to cause a reaction, to create something explosive and intense, something to take your breath away. He grinned at the thought, shifting the angle of his head, and he heard her breath catch.

"That's…that's good," she said.

"You like it when things explode?" he asked, raising an eyebrow teasingly.

"No, I mean that look. That's good. Hold that." The clicking got louder as she took shot after shot. By this point, he was mostly able to ignore the camera. He focused on the woman behind it, on the blush that the equipment wasn't quite able to hide. Maybe the hat wasn't a bad idea after all. Not if it made her flush so prettily.

She cleared her throat. "Angle the hat back a bit, let me see more of your face."

"Like this, sweetheart?" he asked, adjusting the hat and cocking out his hip to emphasize the line of his bared torso. He wasn't good only with bombs. He knew how to use chemistry in all *sorts* of fun ways. And he was well aware of how women responded to him, how to make their attraction spike and flare. Maybe it would even help him garner the information he was there to find. If he could get her to open up to him, to trust him, she could be the key to finding the intel he needed.

Seducing the data out of a beautiful blonde sounded like a hell of a lot more fun than breaking into offices after dark.

Grab your copy of **Gage (SEAL Team Ten Book One)** from www.LeslieNorthBooks.com